TIMO PARVELA

BICYCLING TO THE MOON

ILLUSTRATED BY VIRPI TALVITIE
TRANSLATED BY RUTH URBOM

GECKO PRESS

This edition first published in 2016 by Gecko Press
PO Box 9335, Marion Square, Wellington 6141, New Zealand
info@geckopress.com

English language edition © Gecko Press Ltd 2016

First American edition published in 2016 by Gecko Press USA, an imprint of Gecko Press Ltd

Text © Timo Parvela
Illustrations © Virpi Talvitie
English translation © Ruth Urbom
Original title: *Maukka ja Väykkä*
First published in Finnish by Tammi in 2009
Published by arrangement with Werner Söderström Ltd (WSOY), Finland

Distributed in the United States and Canada by Lerner Publishing Group, www.lernerbooks.com
Distributed in the United Kingdom by Bounce Sales and Marketing, www.bouncemarketing.co.uk
Distributed in Australia by Scholastic Australia, www.scholastic.com.au
Distributed in New Zealand by Upstart Distribution, www.upstartpress.co.nz

The publisher gratefully acknowledges the Finnish Literature Exchange
for assistance with translation and publication costs.

F I
L I

Edited by Penelope Todd
Design and typesetting by Katrina Duncan
Printed in China by Everbest Printing Co Ltd, an accredited ISO 14001 & FSC certified printer

Hardback (USA) ISBN: 978-1-776570-31-7
Paperback ISBN: 978-1-776570-32-4
Ebook available

For more curiously good books, visit www.geckopress.com

CONTENTS

BICYCLING TO THE MOON

 Purdy and Barker were friends who lived in a sky-blue house on top of a hill. The blue had been Purdy's choice. He loved the sky. He loved puffy white clouds, dark rain clouds, and thin wispy clouds. Above all, he loved the moon and the silver path it made across the lake at the bottom of the hill.

"The moon is so beautiful. If only I could go there, I'd never wish for anything else," Purdy sighed.

Barker didn't say anything. He was already asleep, tired out from the day's work.

Barker was dreaming about their little farm. He loved the fresh smells of earth, grass, and muddy country roads. He loved sunrise and the scent of a new day. Every day he dug in the vegetable garden and planted another row of potatoes. Every evening he came back covered in soil and dust. Purdy wouldn't let him in until he'd swum in the lake for fear he'd dirty everything inside. Barker hated swimming; he couldn't stand water. Tonight as usual he'd gone down obediently to the edge of the lake, then stared at the dark water without dipping so much as a paw in. Then he went home, as dirty as before.

"This is as clean as I could get," Barker growled.

"You're not even wet," Purdy said.

"The water was dry," Barker sniffed, climbing into his crate to go to sleep.

Time passed.

One day Purdy said, "I want a bicycle."

"Is that so?" Barker said.

He knew very well that Purdy was always longing for something. Once a rosy-red hammock, another time a boat with a yellow sail.

One time Purdy wished for a music box.

"If I have a music box, I'll never wish for anything else in my life. I'm sure it'll make me a better friend, too. When I open my music box every evening, it will play for you and we'll live happily ever after," Purdy promised.

Barker used all his savings to buy a music box as a birthday surprise for his friend. When Purdy opened the present, he gave the key one turn.

"It's nice, but not exactly as I imagined." He put the music box on the windowsill, where it remains to this day.

So Barker didn't take much notice of Purdy's longing for a bike. He didn't long for anything, himself. Barker wanted only to dig, to scratch up the earth and turn it over. That was enough.

But Purdy was persistent.

"If I had a bike, I could ride along that silver path all the way to the moon," he said wistfully.

"You wouldn't be able to pedal all that way," said Barker.

"I'd build up speed going down the hill," said Purdy.

"You can't ride a bike on a moonbeam path."

"Have you ever tried?" Purdy asked.

"You don't even know how to ride a bike in the first place." Barker ended the conversation.

Purdy would have added, "Well, I could learn, if only I had a bike," but Barker had already gone back to his work.

Purdy wouldn't leave Barker in peace, all that day, or the next.

"If I get a bicycle, I'll never, ever ask for another thing," Purdy promised, as Barker thinned the carrot patch.

"If I make it to the moon, I'll be a better cat and a better friend," Purdy said, as Barker carried firewood into the kitchen.

"I bet it's really beautiful on the moon. You can see the whole Earth from there—and this hill, with our sky-blue house on top. Once I've seen it, I'll definitely come back the happiest cat in the world, to the prettiest house in the world, and I'll never want anything else ever again. Never, ever," Purdy sighed.

Barker carried on sealing up the windows. After summer came autumn, then in winter the wind would sneak through any gaps in the windows.

At harvest time, Barker pulled up the potatoes and carrots. He picked apples and made them into apple sauce. He made juice from berries and ground grain into flour. Anything left over he took to the autumn market.

Once the last bottle of juice was sold, Barker was pleased. He had earned enough money to buy a new hoe or even a new wheelbarrow. That's what Barker was dreaming about when he saw the bicycle. It was silver like the moon path, with big wheels and a shiny bell. It cost an awful lot: as much as a wheelbarrow and definitely more than the best hoe.

Barker bought the bicycle for Purdy without knowing why. He didn't actually believe anyone could ride up the moon path on a bike. But just like that, without batting an eyelid, he spent all he'd earned on a bike for Purdy to ride to the moon.

"Bicycling to the moon—as if! Pfft. This'll teach him. That cat's going to land in the pond with a plop. Always telling me to wash. Well, he's about to learn his lesson," Barker muttered as he wheeled the bike home.

Purdy was beside himself with joy over the bike. For a whole month he tried diligently to master riding it. Barker watched from the garden swing as Purdy wobbled this way and that. Every so often Purdy crashed into the side of the barn. Then he rode straight through the sheets on the clothesline and into the compost heap. For the most part, Purdy just tried to stay on his bike.

After a month, Purdy could circle the garden swing without falling off.

"There's a full moon tonight," he said.

Barker only nodded.

The disc of the moon glowed in the night sky. The silver pathway shimmered invitingly on the lake. Purdy sat on his bike outside the sky-blue house on the hill. Barker stood beside him, looking serious.

"Well, here I go," Purdy said. "First I'll build up speed down the hill, then I'll jump onto the moonbeam path and pedal all the way to the moon."

"I'll wave to you from here," Barker promised.

Purdy sat silently on his bike, looking down towards the lake. The silver pathway was brighter than ever. It led from the lake shore right up to the moon.

"But what if it doesn't work? What if I veer off the path and end up in the lake?" Purdy wondered.

Barker said nothing. That's exactly what he was hoping for. He'd waited all month for this, and soon he'd have a good laugh at his friend's expense.

"I can't swim," Purdy said.

"You can't?" Barker asked in surprise. Although he detested water, he was actually a good swimmer.

"No. Well, I guess I'll just try to stay on the path," Purdy said casually.

Barker was quiet. He sighed deeply as Purdy got ready to set off.

"Wait," Barker said. "I'll go with you."

"Why?" Purdy asked.

"Because we're friends," Barker said.

So they both got on the bike and off they went. Purdy steered and Barker sat on the rack. Faster and faster they sped. The dark lake approached at a furious pace. Up ahead, the silver path gleamed like a runway. When they hit the shoreline, the bicycle took off. It glided up the silver path towards the moon that shone above. The bike rose and rose, until it swerved and plunged into the lake, shattering the moonbeam path into a thousand pieces. Then the surface became calm again. There was complete silence, until two figures suddenly popped up. Barker hauled his best buddy Purdy to shore while the bike sank into the dark depths of the lake.

Purdy and Barker clambered up to the sky-blue house on the hill. They sat in the garden swing and gazed at the incredibly beautiful full moon.

"Good thing you wanted to come along, or I'm sure I would have drowned," Purdy said.

"Yes, indeed," said Barker.

"It was silly to think we could ride up that path to the moon," Purdy said. After a moment, he added, "I think we were too heavy together. It might work if we each had our own bike. Two bikes."

Barker just laughed.

A GOOD LOSER

 Purdy loved games. He loved chess, Monopoly, badminton, volleyball, football, and handball, and he certainly would have liked backball, headball, and shoulderball too, if those games existed. Yes, Purdy loved playing games; what he hated was losing.

Barker was weeding the vegetable garden. He bent down towards a row of carrots, closed one eye, and pawed out the weeds by their roots. The carrots were in tidy rows, like all the other vegetables he grew: radishes, lettuces, peas, and beans. The vegetable garden was Barker's pride and joy, so he was far from delighted when the ball landed smack in the middle of the lettuce patch.

"I'm trying out my spin kick," Purdy said.

"Go and try it somewhere else. I'm weeding," Barker grumbled as he handed the ball back to Purdy.

"You could come and have a kick with me. We could play a friendly match."

"We're friends without having to play matches," Barker snorted. "At least we were a minute ago," he added as he tidied up the lettuces.

"Don't be a spoilsport. Playing is fun and it peps you up," Purdy said, but Barker had already gone to fetch what he needed to make a scarecrow.

He gathered various items and old clothes on the lawn and was wondering how to dress the scarecrow when the ball hit him on the head.

"I'm trying out my goal kick," Purdy said.

"Go and try it somewhere else. I'm making a scarecrow to keep the birds away. Maybe I need a scare-cat as well," Barker grumbled as he handed the ball back.

"You could be goalie. It's boring playing on my own."

"I've got work to do. I don't have time."

"Not even for a little match? I promise I won't bother you again if you come and have a tiny play."

Barker gave a deep sigh. He looked at his work, then at Purdy, whose eyes gleamed with excitement. He carefully leaned his hoe against the house and followed Purdy into the front yard.

Purdy had already set up old buckets for goalposts. He was bouncing the ball impatiently.

"Five minutes," Barker said. "Then I'm going back to my work."

"It's the big friendly match of the season: Purdy versus Barker," Purdy announced, then put the ball into play, even though Barker was still hanging his hat on a branch.

Purdy kicked the ball between the buckets. "Goooal! Goooal!" he whooped. "Purdy's in the lead: one–nil."

"I wasn't even ready," Barker grumbled.

"Oh, don't worry about losing. It's just a game," Purdy said.

"How come my goal is twice as wide as yours?" Barker asked.

"You're upset because I'm a better player than you," Purdy said, placing the ball for kick-off.

Barker was just about to kick off when Purdy pointed at the house. "Hey, the porch roof could do with a new coat of paint," he said.

"How could it? I've just painted it." Barker turned to look. The porch roof was nice and red, the paintwork smooth. As he looked, Purdy booted the ball into the goal.

"He shoots and scores! Two–nil!" Purdy shrieked.

"You cheated," Barker said.

The match carried on like that. When Barker stumbled, Purdy claimed a free kick. If Barker managed to kick the ball, Purdy screamed "Offside!" and "Send him to the penalty box!"

"As far as I know, players don't get sent to the penalty box in this game," Barker said. While he sat out his penalty on the garden swing, Purdy scored six goals.

"Which of us knows this game better?" Purdy asked.

"You do."

"But you didn't even cheer my great goals," Purdy complained.

After the final minute of play, the score was Purdy 60, Barker 0.

"I know it bothers you, losing to me," Purdy said. He tried to sound sympathetic, but his purr gave him away.

"I'm not bothered," Barker said.

"Of course you're bothered. Admit it."

"Not at all. It was only a game."

"Shall we have a rematch? I'll make it a bit easier for you this time."

Barker didn't reply. He took his hat from the branch and returned to his jobs, while Purdy turned cartwheels to celebrate his victory.

That evening, Barker sat on the porch, enjoying some delicious, sweet juice at the end of a hot day. He had made the juice himself from berries he'd picked last autumn. There were still a dozen or so bottles in the cellar, plenty to last until this year's crop ripened. The new scarecrow stood at the edge of the vegetable garden. Even in its ragged clothes, it looked impressive in the evening sun.

Purdy, on the other hand, looked awfully glum as he wandered around the yard. He peered under the berry bushes, behind the shed, and even among the rhubarb plants. Finally he gave up and came to sit on the porch next to Barker.

"Have you seen my ball?" he asked.

"Oh yes, I've seen it," Barker said.

"Where?"

"In my goal. Sixty times."

"Oh yeah." The memory made Purdy smile. "Sounds like you're still upset about that match."

"Not at all."

"It takes a lot of effort to be as good a player as me," Purdy said. "And I have to admit, I admire you in a way. There aren't many who'd take a defeat as calmly as you, Barker. You're the best loser I know."

"Thanks," Barker said.

"Too bad my ball's gone missing. Otherwise we could play an evening friendly match, which you could lose again."

Barker said nothing. The rays of the setting sun shone on the scarecrow, whose head somehow resembled Purdy's ball. Barker leaned back in his chair and smiled to himself, the smile of a winner.

TERRIBLE WEATHER

Perfect! Winky Pig gazed at her reflection in the mirror. She tilted her head and stretched her neck. Her pearl necklace was exquisite. Winky gave a quiet squeal.

The weather outside was gorgeous. The sun was shining, and summer was at its peak. The gleaming clouds were almost a match for Winky's necklace.

Winky went over to Henny Cluckington's house and knocked on the door.

"Hello," she said.

At first, Henny said nothing. She didn't seem pleased to see her unexpected visitor.

Winky searched for something to say. "Lovely weather."

"Terrible. On days like this everyone should stay home," Henny replied.

"I wondered if you'd like to come for a walk," Winky said.

"I bought six new coffee cups last month, each with a gold band around the rim," said Henny.

"How delightful," Winky said.

"I got six silver teaspoons with the cups. Also six saucers and six dessert plates—a total of twelve plates, six cups, and six spoons. Twenty-four items in all. So I have a twenty-four-piece set."

"Lovely," Winky said. "Do you drink coffee from your new cups?"

"They're only for special occasions." Henny sounded irritated. "I see no reason to celebrate. Besides, I'm in the middle of cleaning the front hall."

"Oh, sorry," Winky said, and left her to it.

"The nerve! Dressing up and thinking she's somebody special. Coming to other people's homes and talking only about herself," Henny sniffed when Winky had gone.

But Winky wasn't put off. A light breeze caressed her snout, and dust puffed up between her trotters.

Next she knocked on Daisy Butterfield's door. The top half of the door opened, and a head with horns poked out. Daisy chewed, deep in thought, as she looked at the pig on her front porch.

"Is something the matter?" she asked.

"Not at all," Winky said.

"Well then. There you go. Aren't you going to catch a cold in this awful weather?"

"It's not awful at all. Come on, let's go for a walk."

"Not likely! If I were you, I'd be putting on boots, not pearls." Daisy slammed the door shut.

Nothing could spoil Winky's good mood. She went on to ask Martha Woollaston, Connie Quackstrom, and Cloppity Hay to go for a walk, but they all thought the weather was too miserable.

Finally Winky headed up to Purdy and Barker's house. It took some effort, climbing all the way up the hill. At last, she stood at their door, out of breath, and knocked with her trotter. Barker was out fishing, so Purdy came to the door.

"Lovely weather today," Winky said.

"So I've heard," Purdy said mysteriously.

"I've asked everyone to come for a walk, but nobody wants to," Winky said.

"So I've heard," Purdy said again.

"Would you like to come?" Winky asked.

"I have visitors at the moment. Another time," Purdy said, closing the door.

Winky Pig stood there, not knowing what to do. She had run out of animals to ask. Maybe the weather was terrible after all, although the sun was so hot she'd have taken off her coat if she had one on.

Just as she was turning for home, laughter came from inside the house. Carefully, Winky climbed onto an upturned tub and peeped in through a window. In the front room were Henny Cluckington, Daisy Butterfield, Martha Woollaston, Connie

Quackstrom, Cloppity Hay, and a few others. They were all laughing at Purdy, who wore a necklace made of raisins.

"I bet it is," Winky heard someone say. And everyone laughed again.

"Lovely weather today," said Barker, coming up the hill with five plump perch he had caught.

"Miserable," Winky said.

"Is it?" Barker looked up at the cloudless sky.

"Nobody should go out for a walk in this weather," Winky said, hanging her head.

"I see. But that's a beautiful pearl necklace you're wearing," Barker said.

"Do you think so?"

"Sure. It's really pretty."

"Thank you. It's a birthday present from my mother. Today's my birthday," Winky said.

"Then we should celebrate," Barker said, and he went to fetch the fish smoker from the shed.

The evening sun cast a beautiful golden light over the yard as Barker and Winky feasted on the tasty smoked fish. Winky breathed in the delicious smoky scent that hung in the air. Meanwhile, Purdy and the others waited indoors for the clouds to clear and grumbled about weather so rotten they could smell it inside.

FISHING

 Purdy liked fishing, but he hated where the fish lived. The lake was not only deep and dark, it was also wet. That's why fishing had always been Barker's job. Barker didn't like the water either, and wasn't an enthusiastic angler, but fishing and casting nets in the gentle evening sunlight made a pleasant change from garden work. The catch was usually small fry—a few tiddlers on the hook and a couple of decent-sized fish in the net—but that was enough for a tasty dinner.

One day Purdy wanted to go fishing, too. He had got his paws on a book entitled *All About Fishing (and a Few Other Things Besides)*. Being a keen reader, he had finished the whole book in one sitting. He got excited and studied even more books about fish. Now he was absolutely convinced that Barker was fishing all wrong. With two nets and one fishing rod, he ought to be catching loads more fish. Purdy saw with his own eyes pictures of all the lovely pike, perch, whitefish, salmon, and trout they hadn't been eating, since Barker clearly didn't know the first thing about fishing. In the end Purdy was so bothered about missing out on those tasty delicacies he decided to defy his natural fear of water and instruct his friend in the fine art of fishing—at which he now considered himself a master.

Barker raised his eyebrows as Purdy packed six fish books into his backpack, along with a nautical chart, a compass, his passport, a box of fishing tackle, sandwiches, more sandwiches, a fishing net, and a barometer.

"We're only going down to the lake," Barker said.

"Yes, I know." Purdy added a seventh book to his backpack.

"We'll only be there for an hour or two," Barker said.

"Sure." Purdy groaned as he tried to lift his backpack.

"We don't need anything. The fishing rod is already down there. So are the nets," Barker said.

Purdy said nothing more. He couldn't actually speak under the weight of his backpack, which was squashing him.

"Thanks," Purdy puffed when Barker lifted the backpack off him. "Maybe I'll leave the compass here."

Finally the two friends made it to the lake shore, where Barker parked the wheelbarrow carrying both Purdy and his backpack.

"Of course, I would have walked, only I sprained my front paw on the backpack," Purdy explained.

The lake was completely calm. Insects flicked over its surface as if being whisked about on invisible strings. Rising fish made rings in the dark water and a gull cried somewhere in the distance.

"Excellent fishing weather," Purdy declared, raising a paw to check the wind direction.

"Actually, a west wind would be better."

Barker had already put his net into the boat, which he was about to push out.

"Stop, stop, stop! What on earth are you doing?" Purdy asked in horror.

"I thought I'd put the nets among the reeds, as always," Barker explained. "Then I'll sit in the boat and fish for half an hour or so, bring up the nets, clean the fish, and go back up to make our dinner. Fried perch, probably."

"That's not how you do it. First you have to check the season, the temperature and texture of the water, wind direction, type of lake bed and pressure in the air. Only then can we plan what we're going to fish for and how."

"Sounds complicated," Barker muttered, glancing at the lake as a good-sized fish leaped to the surface.

"It only sounds that way. Trust me," Purdy said.

Barker positioned the boat on the shore and waited while Purdy took measurements. He watched as Purdy dug out the books, barometer, calculator, and a big notebook with graph paper, in which he started to draw a careful diagram of the lake. Purdy strode around the lake, counting his steps. He wrote the number in his notebook, measured angles, observed the sky, felt the water and evaluated its texture, taste, and smell. Time passed. The lake grew quiet, the fish rings disappeared, and a thin mist formed over the surface. The moon rose, and still Purdy measured, drew, calculated, and diagrammed.

Barker woke up with a start. He had fallen asleep and slid into the bottom of the boat. For a moment he didn't know where he was but, seeing Purdy's whiskery face, he remembered.

"Stop snoring. You're scaring the fish away," Purdy hissed.

"What time is it, anyway?" Barker asked.

"According to my calculations, it's exactly the right time. Not too late and not too soon," Purdy replied. "We'll put the nets in now."

"Wouldn't it be better to go to bed? We can come back tomorrow and put them in then."

"Then I'd have to start all over. Right now should be ideal." Purdy pushed the boat into the water.

Barker rowed silently as Purdy directed. Three strokes with the left oar, two with the right, slow down. Three strokes with the right oar, two more, back with the right.

"Now," Purdy said, "we're in precisely the right spot."

And so they lowered the nets. And waited and waited. The moon passed over the lake, the treetops grew lighter, and the mist began to lift.

"Now," Purdy said.

Barker took hold of one net and started hauling it into the boat. It was heavy and glistened underwater. Purdy had to help because there was no way Barker could lift the net, which was

bursting with fish. The bottom of the boat was already flopping, bouncing, and teeming with perch, whitefish, roach, ruffe, and zander, and more kept coming as they brought in the net. Purdy and Barker got hot and sweaty dragging the fish up. The boat was getting lower and lower in the water.

When they finally had the nets hauled in, Barker had a tough job rowing back to shore. Purdy had to sit right out in front on the bow. He looked down in horror at the water, which was nearly up to the edge of the boat.

"Well, what do you say?" Purdy asked, bursting with pride once they had their fully laden boat onshore.

"Big job," Barker said.

"Yes, it was," Purdy sighed.

"What do you mean 'was'?" Barker asked.

"It's over now. We've landed our catch, and now you can thank me for teaching you how to fish properly."

"I'll thank you later, when all these fish have been gutted. Now that's a big job," Barker said.

"Oh, I hadn't thought of that."

"And when we've gutted them all, we'll have to figure out what to do with them. We don't have enough storage space for them all, or a big enough pan. If we cook them in small batches we'll be done by next Wednesday evening. I suggest we share some with our friends and sell the rest at the market. If we start right away, we might be finished in half a day," Barker explained.

Purdy said nothing. He looked in horror at the thrashing mound in the nets. He glanced at the sun, already peeping over the hill. He gulped, went over to the nets, took out a fish and chucked it into the lake.

For hours, Purdy and Barker took fish from the nets and released them into the water, until only two decent-sized fish and a few tiddlers were left in the bottom of the boat. Barker gutted them and gathered them up. The exhausted anglers trudged up the hill with the sun blazing high in the sky.

The backpack with the damp fishing books stayed down by the lake until Purdy finally went back to fetch it in late autumn.

A GOOD DAY

 Barker woke first. The room was still dark, but a thin streak of light sliced through the curtains and onto the floor. That's how Barker knew the day had begun. He knew in other ways too— more precisely by smelling. Even before he opened his eyes, he sniffed the air and took in the morning: the scent of flowers opening, of dew and fresh earth. He also heard the insects.

Barker slowly stretched his left paw, then his right. He stretched his hind legs and curled his tail. Then he got up. Purdy, meanwhile, burrowed deeper under the covers.

Barker picked up the red bucket he had placed in the doorway the night before. Outside it was a bit chilly, but soon the sun would warm the path to the well, which Barker padded along

NS PL

*** TRANSIT SLIP ***
** DISCHARGE ON
ARRIVAL ***

Author: Parvela, Timo,
Title: Bicycling to the Moon
Item ID: 1804869137
Transit to: NSPL
User ID 0212889098

to fetch water. The winch above the well squeaked as he turned it. When he'd pulled up the full bucket, Barker went to get an oil can from the shed and squirted a bit on the ends of the winch axle. Now the winch turned silently. Barker smiled in satisfaction.

He made a fire and placed a beat-up pan on the stove. The fire had its own smell. It was a mixture of smoke, burning wood, and something Barker couldn't identify: the smell of fire. While he waited for the coffee, he made himself three large sausage sandwiches. The sausages smelled delicious and meaty. He also made two triangular sardine sandwiches for Purdy's breakfast, covered them with a second plate, and placed them on the table.

Barker opened a curtain, filling the room with soft morning light. Or half the room, rather, because he considerately left Purdy's half dark.

Barker sat and munched on his sandwich. He poured coffee into a big blue mug. For a moment he didn't even touch it because the coffee smelled so irresistibly good. He took a deep whiff with his eyes shut.

"Stop that racket," Purdy growled from underneath his pile of covers.

Barker simply smiled and took a sip.

Purdy didn't get up until Barker was ready to go out. He opened one eye in the dark and poked his head from under the covers. Barker was taking his work gloves off the nail by the door. Purdy tried to recall whether he had promised to do anything in particular today. Perhaps. He had the feeling he had. Then he felt tired again and snoozed for another half hour.

Later, Purdy sat bleary-eyed at the table, watching through the window as Barker tied up the pea plants in the vegetable garden. His sardine sandwiches were warm from the sun. Purdy took a bite and chewed reluctantly. The ticking of the clock annoyed him.

The sun rose over the shed, over the birch tree in the yard, and higher still, until nothing was left in the shade beneath its warm gaze. Barker finished with the pea patch and went over to cut down the nettles by the shed so they couldn't spread and grow all over the place. On the way he noticed the clothesline badly needed replacing.

Purdy dragged himself out of the house around midday. The sun dazzled his sensitive eyes, which immediately fell on the pile of logs beside the meadow. He had promised to move them into the shed to dry. He looked hopefully at the sky, but there were no rain clouds to save him.

Purdy carried one log into the shed. Barker was scything the nettles in strong, even strokes.

Purdy carried in another log.

In the afternoon they sat together on the porch, drinking coffee that Barker had made. Barker watched a pied flycatcher carrying in its beak a dragonfly almost as big as itself. The bird couldn't make the dragonfly fit through the hole in its tree. Purdy stared gloomily at the woodpile, which hadn't shrunk one bit. They had spoon cookies and S-shaped cinnamon cookies with their coffee. Barker liked both almost equally.

Later that afternoon, a gray cloud appeared and advanced

towards the house. It started raining just as Barker was finishing his jobs. Purdy hadn't made a proper start on his.

It was only a light shower, but it lasted almost an hour. Barker made good use of the time and went to buy a new clothesline.

Purdy made good use of the time, too: he wrapped himself in a quilt to watch the rain. The woodpile turned shiny gray in the wet.

Barker fried up leftover boiled potatoes for dinner, along with fresh eggs from the store.

Henny Cluckington came round that evening to borrow three detective novels from Purdy. She gossiped about Winky Pig and her new pearl necklace.

"Pearls for swine," Purdy snorted.

"You said it," Henny added.

"Mm-hm," said Purdy.

"I'll be off then. I'm sure you have plenty to do."

"I was just thinking about a song."

"Oh, some people have so many talents. Well, it was lovely to chat. Thank you for the books. I'll bring them back when I've read them."

"No rush. I've read them, and Barker hardly ever reads," Purdy said, with a meaningful look at Barker, who was fixing the handle of his hammer.

"Some people never get anything done," Henny said.

"You said it," Purdy said.

After Henny left, Barker went out to cover the woodpile so it wouldn't get even wetter if it rained in the night. Then he washed his face, made an evening cup of tea, and went to bed feeling pleased.

"That was a good day," Barker mumbled as he dropped off to sleep.

Purdy sat on the porch for a while. His eyes gleamed in the dark, and his whiskers quivered. He heard a field mouse squeak in the meadow and the high-pitched squeaks of bats in the attic. He watched a daddy-long-legs bustling along, searching for prey in the cracks between boards. Somewhere a hedgehog snuffled. The night was full of small, delicate sounds that made Purdy purr softly.

At the very darkest hour of the night, the first lines of a song came to him:

Uncanny flashes: cat's eyes in the night.
A log pile creaks and trembles,
a cat's chest quivers and rumbles.
Summer, and the night is still young.

When it began to grow light, Purdy crawled happily under the covers.

"It came to me in the end. It was a good day," he purred.

THE GREAT TOMATO WAR

 Sometimes Purdy and Barker squabbled, but mostly they were peace-loving creatures. Neither ever wanted to harm the other, much less start a fight or declare war. Once in a while, though, war breaks out, even though neither side wants it. It's a pity, but that's how it is. And that's what happened one Friday in late summer, when the great tomato war was waged.

Barker had been tending his tomatoes since early spring. He had made a little greenhouse from old window panes, supported the seedlings with sticks, watered them and got rid of any pests. By summer, the little green tomato buds had ripened into big round red globes that hung heavy on the plants. Every morning Barker went around gently feeling how ripe they were and measuring to find the biggest tomato. He planned to take it to the vegetable show, where the biggest, juiciest vegetable would win a prize. Barker was sure to be the winner because his tomatoes were so magnificent.

On that fateful Friday morning Barker was certain this was the day his tomatoes would finally be ripe enough. They had to be, because the show was that weekend. Whistling a jaunty tune, Barker took out his measuring tape and sent Purdy off to work on his jigsaw puzzle. Purdy had spent most of the summer working on a huge 10,000-piece puzzle. He was sure today was the day he would finish it.

It was sunny, with a slight smell of smoke in the air. The dry late-summer weather had turned the grass brown, but the climate inside the greenhouse was perfect for tomatoes. They were big, red, and plump. Barker breathed in a lungful of tomato-scented air and went over to his biggest specimen. It was slightly hidden beneath lush green leaves in the sunniest corner of the greenhouse. Barker smiled as he parted the leaves.

"Good morning, my plump little beauty," he said. But where the tomato had hung, there was only a bare stem.

Barker stepped back. His head was spinning, and he couldn't take in what he had just seen—or rather, what he hadn't seen. He looked around the greenhouse as if he had never been there before. Then he went back to the door, carefully checked which direction he was facing, took the same two steps he took every morning over to the tomato, and parted the leaves. The tomato had vanished.

As he ran back to the house, Barker saw tomato-red. He was

absolutely certain Purdy had taken it. Purdy was jealous that Barker would soon win great tomato glory at the vegetable show.

"Where's my tomato?" Barker shouted as he went inside. "What have you done with it?" he bellowed, leaning on the table with his paws on Purdy's jigsaw puzzle.

"Be careful of my puzzle. It's nearly finished."

"You ate my tomato!" Barker said.

"How can you get so worked up over a single tomato? You've got a whole greenhouse full of them."

"Where's my tomato?" Barker roared.

Then Purdy and Barker glared at each other, motionless, the way cats and dogs sometimes do. Barker bared his teeth on the left side and growled, and Purdy's tail fur bristled to three times its size.

"All right," Purdy said finally, slightly afraid. "It's there in the kitchen."

Barker sprang into the kitchen. There was a moment's silence. Purdy listened tensely. Then there was an almighty yelp that made the rest of Purdy's fur stand on end.

"I can explain," he stammered when Barker returned with a dish of tomato pulp. "I thought we could celebrate my finishing the jigsaw puzzle. I was going to make spaghetti with homemade tomato sauce. You've always loved it before."

Without a word, Barker tipped the whole dish of pulped tomato over Purdy's puzzle.

"My jigsaw! You've ruined it!" Purdy yelled as he tried to wipe off the tomato. It was no use. The blue sky had turned tomato-red. The castle in the middle of the picture was red and the knight in the foreground—the bit Purdy liked best—was as red as… well, as a tomato.

Purdy leaped up and ran out the door. Fearing the worst, Barker dashed after him, but he was too late. He got the first tomato in his face when he reached the greenhouse door. Barker recoiled, grabbed three tomatoes from the nearest plant, and fired them one by one at Purdy's head. Purdy responded with a torrent of tomatoes, and Barker had to duck behind the nearest row of plants.

The battle was short but destructive. Afterwards not a single tomato was left, only a red cat and a red dog sitting glumly among the smashed tomatoes. Their fur was mucky with drying tomato pulp, and as their rage subsided they felt a bit mucky themselves.

"Sorry," Purdy said, swallowing a sob.

"Sorry," Barker said, wiping away tears and tomato.

"I didn't know that was your best tomato," said Purdy.

Barker didn't say anything. He was annoyed. What annoyed him most was that if only he had paused to think right at the start, he would have realized that his second-biggest tomato could have won the big prize. But a war can't be stopped, and you can't undo it afterwards. So there was nothing Purdy and Barker could do except calm down, wash off in the lake, and make an enormous batch of delicious tomato sauce for dinner, which they invited some friends over to share. And that evening, in the flickering candlelight, it occurred to Barker that tomatoes certainly taste better in sauce than on a competition judge's table. Purdy wasn't too upset about his red jigsaw puzzle, either. Especially when everyone was amazed that he had managed to put together such a huge puzzle with nothing but red.

THE GREAT MUSHROONY HUNT

 After all the crops had been harvested and the soil turned over in preparation for spring, Barker didn't have much to do. Mostly he just stared out and sighed. Sometimes he went out to tidy the firewood in the shed, but it had already been organized by size, length, and type of wood. If a single leaf fell from a tree, Barker rushed out to rake it up, but autumn was not very long and there were only a few leaves left to fall.

Barker wasn't unhappy, oh no, but he was a dog. And a dog ought to carry things, bury them, dig them up, and take them somewhere else. A dog ought to be doing something, and that's the feeling Barker had, like an itch that never went away no matter how much he scratched it.

"Stop that scratching and sighing," Purdy snapped. "I'm trying to concentrate."

"But you're not doing anything," Barker said in surprise.

Purdy was lounging in an armchair, which he had moved into the middle of the room to catch the sun. He hadn't budged since that morning, when he'd got out of bed and settled into the chair.

"I'm concentrating."

"What are you concentrating on?"

"I don't know yet. There are so many things waiting to be done."

"Tell me what they are and I'll take care of them. Where shall I start?" Barker was excited.

"I don't know what they are yet."

"How can that be?"

"They haven't been thought up yet."

"How can you be concentrating on something that doesn't exist?" Barker asked impatiently.

"Well, I can't if you keep bugging me."

Purdy went back to concentrating on concentrating, while Barker sulked. Then he started cleaning the floor, which he had just mopped the day before, and the day before, and the day before that.

"Very well," Purdy sighed when Barker kept banging the broom against the chair legs until he couldn't concentrate on anything else. "I'm thinking about mushroonies."

"Mushroonies? Do you mean mushrooms?" Barker said.

"I mean mushroonies. Big, juicy mushroonies that set off around this time of year for the mushroony valley, where they'll spend the winter."

"Why are you thinking about them now?"

"Because this is exactly the time we should head for the mushroony forest."

"Is it really?" Barker yelped in excitement, and put the broom away.

"Yes. Nothing's tastier on a chilly autumn evening than mushroony hash," Purdy said.

Out in the forest, Barker started digging. His paws shifted the earth like two turbocharged machines. The hole was already so deep you could only see his tail sticking out, but still he kept digging. He wanted to make sure not a single tender, tasty mushroony escaped once they'd fallen into his trap.

Purdy had chosen a bend in the path for his trap, beside a big lumpy boulder. He could lie in wait there once the hole was finished. Besides, the hole was close to their house. So close that Purdy managed to wheel his armchair out into the sun behind the boulder—a great place to wait for a herd of mushroonies to come stampeding along the path.

"Stampeding?" Barker asked from the hole, which was now so deep his voice sounded distant and muffled. It also sounded a bit worried. "Are mushroonies so big their feet thunder?"

"They might," Purdy said.

Barker's anxious nose poked out of the hole.

"How big are these mushroonies meant to be?" he asked.

"Maybe the size of a shrub, maybe as big as a house. I'm not sure."

"How come you're not sure?"

"Because I've never seen one," Purdy said a little impatiently.

That made Barker think. He imagined mushroonies the size of a house thundering down the path and making the earth shudder. He pictured huge, disgruntled mushroonies that took exception to the hole that Barker had dug in the middle of their path.

Suddenly Barker wasn't sure he even liked mushroony hash. Its tastiness began to seem highly overrated.

"Maybe we've been a little hasty," Barker said tentatively.

"How do you mean?" Purdy asked.

"We haven't worked out what to do with the mushroonies if we catch them. Where will we keep so many of them?"

"Good question," Purdy said. "I hadn't thought of that."

"We'll need a bigger kitchen and a lot of new pots and pans."

"Sounds like a lot of trouble," Purdy said.

"And then some. We need to make sure everything's ready first."

"What about this hole?"

"We'll have to fill it in, of course. We don't want to reveal our plan too soon." Barker started filling the hole with dirt again.

Barker spent all autumn building a big mushroony storage hut in the far corner of the garden. It turned out very sturdy and fine, and Barker didn't even mind that mushroony season was over by the time it was finished. Next autumn everything would be ready when the mushroonies began their great migration. Besides, building the hut was a good way to spend the autumn, and it fit nicely between the storage huts for crabbages and plumkins.

A DAY OFF

Even Barker couldn't be bothered some days. Sometimes he simply felt lazy; other times it was irresistible to behave like a dog. He felt like digging a hole for no reason at all. He wanted to bury things he had no intention of digging up later. He chewed on a boot or the fingers of a glove, just for fun. Yes, at the end of the day, Barker was, after all, a dog.

One autumn morning Barker smelled something. He had just finished raking leaves into piles under the apple trees and was going to fetch the wheelbarrow from the shed when a peculiar scent reached his nostrils. The crisp air was filled with an irresistible tang that made Barker so restless he had to let out a howl. He raised his muzzle and gave first a short howl, then a longer one. The sound rose up like a sword piercing the peaceful air. Daisy Butterfield stopped eating her porridge, Henny Cluckington laid a square egg, and even the smoke seemed to freeze in the chimneys as the howl reverberated through the morning.

Purdy raced outside, eyes wide. He was even more startled to see Barker, who sat in a pile of leaves and howled with his eyes closed.

"Have you hurt your paw?" Purdy asked.

Barker glanced over with sad eyes, raised his muzzle, and let out another howl.

Purdy covered his ears with his paws. "Stop it!" he yelled, but Barker didn't stop. He gave three more howls before he calmed down a little.

"What is it?" Purdy asked.

"Can't you feel it?" Barker said. His voice sounded uncertain.

"I can only feel a pain in my ears. I think my eardrums just burst."

"It's thrilling and sad at the same time. Tempting and dangerous." Barker tried to describe it, but he couldn't find the words for all he was feeling and smelling.

"Why don't you go back to your raking? It's supposed to get windy this afternoon. Besides, Henny Cluckington and Daisy Butterfield are coming over. They have something important for me. I want the yard looking nice by then."

But sensible words didn't settle Barker as they usually would. He was still restless and his paws tingled. He started digging a hole in the middle of the lawn. He kicked up the soil, and soon Barker disappeared underground, with only the tip of his tail showing.

Purdy didn't know what to do. Dark clouds gathering on the horizon promised wind and possibly a storm. He looked helplessly at the tidy piles of leaves under the trees. They'd all be scattered again if no one took them off to the compost heap. And the visitors would be here any minute. Purdy sighed and went to fetch the wheelbarrow from the shed. From deep inside the hole came a growl.

Purdy parked the wheelbarrow by the first pile of leaves. An ominous silence hung over the yard. Barker had left his hole and gone off somewhere. Purdy took an armful of leaves and put them in the wheelbarrow. There was huffing and puffing from behind the house. Purdy was bending to pick up more leaves when Barker rushed out. He shot across the yard like a cannonball and blasted through the first pile of leaves. Then he ran through the second, third, fourth, and fifth piles. Leaves flew up as if a tornado had struck the yard, and now Barker ran full tilt at the sixth and final pile, just as Purdy took the wheelbarrow over to it.

"Hold it! Halt! Time out!" Purdy stood in front of the pile to block Barker. It was no use. Barker ran Purdy down as if he were a doormat. Then the last pile of leaves flew up, and Barker went on racing around the yard in fits of laughter.

Purdy sat up and looked crossly at the yard so full of leaves you couldn't tell there had been any raking at all. In the sky, the clouds were building a gray wall that rose silently towards Purdy and Barker's hilltop home. And then, as if things weren't bad enough already, Barker climbed a tree. Just like that.

"What on earth are you doing?" Purdy shrieked, but Barker didn't answer. His eyes bulged as he gripped the trunk of the apple tree with his paws. He'd climbed about halfway up. There were still enough leaves on the tree that Purdy could only make out Barker's hind legs and tail.

"Dogs don't climb trees. Someone has to put some sense into you. Come down this instant!" Purdy ordered.

But Barker did no such thing. He howled again. And just then, Purdy saw Daisy and Henny coming up the hill.

"Get down right now!" Purdy shouted. "Our visitors are coming and you're embarrassing me. I'll never be able to show my face again. Do you hear me?"

Purdy tried shaking the tree, but it was too sturdy. He tried throwing a windfall apple at Barker, but nothing worked. And the visitors were practically here.

"Now you stay there and be quiet so they don't notice you, or I'll never forgive you for this," Purdy hissed before rushing over to the visitors. In his hurry, he didn't notice the hole in the middle of the yard and fell straight in.

"Hello, hello. Nice to see you. Let's go inside right away before the storm gets here," Purdy greeted Henny and Daisy as they peeked into the hole.

"Are you planning to bury something here?" Daisy asked as she hoisted Purdy out.

"A dog," Purdy said.

"Do you mean there's a dog buried in there?" Henny said.

"There was, but he didn't stay there," Purdy said grimly, glancing over at the tree where Barker's anxiously wagging tail was just visible. Fortunately he'd stopped howling for now. All going well, nobody would notice the dog in the tree.

"Why don't we go inside?" Purdy said.

"Have you been raking leaves?" Henny indicated the rake and wheelbarrow.

"Yes. Somebody's got to do it," Purdy said.

"But isn't that a dog's job? Where is Barker, anyway?" Daisy asked.

There was a brief silence. Purdy desperately tried to come up with something to say, but he didn't need to say anything because just then the wind arrived. One mighty gust blew the last leaves from the apple tree, leaving only the naked trunk, bare branches, and a hairy dog. Henny and Daisy stared in silence. Then they looked at Purdy, waiting for an explanation.

"I drove him into the tree," Purdy said faintly.

Henny and Daisy glanced at each other, then nodded.

"Well, we're actually here to announce the winner of this year's Animal Equality Award," Henny said.

Daisy added, "This year's award goes to a cat who digs holes, rakes leaves, and drives dogs up trees."

All at once Purdy looked like the cat who got the cream. A whole bucketful.

MIGRATING FOR THE WINTER

 Overhead, the swans made their honking cry as they departed and their wings beat the air. The big birds stood out against the sharp blue sky. Purdy swallowed. He looked at Barker, busy getting ready for winter: covering the firewood, dragging the garden furniture into the shed, servicing the lawnmower, and hanging his bicycle from the ceiling hooks. Purdy's bike was still at the bottom of the lake. The restlessness that had overtaken Barker in early autumn came in handy now as he prepared all the summer things for storage and all the winter things for use.

The wavering line of swans was disappearing over the forest. Purdy stood first on tiptoe, then on a chair, and finally got up on the roof to watch as long as he could. There came a final distant honk, as if something had come adrift, and they were gone.

Purdy sat on the roof for a long while, enjoying the sunset. He saw the village rooftops, thick smoke from Daisy Butterfield's burning leaf pile, and Henny Cluckington as a tiny dot pushing a wheelbarrow.

Summer was being carted off, Purdy thought, laying his head on his paws. It was being burned, locked away in storage, covered with tarpaulins, or made into compost.

After nightfall, when Purdy finally climbed down and went inside, a fire was already burning. Barker sat on the bench, sharpening a knife. He had gathered all the household tools in a box at his feet and was humming to himself as he mended them. A pile of winter clothes, woolly hats, socks, and mittens sat on a chair, waiting for Barker to check them over and mend any holes.

"Could you bring the winter coats down from the attic? I'll see if they're missing any buttons or if the moths have damaged them," Barker said.

"No," Purdy said.

"It would be easier to do it now while there's time. The first snow might fall any day."

"No," Purdy said.

"Fine. Is anything the matter?"

"No."

Purdy crawled into bed and pulled the covers over his head. He was freezing. He shivered at the mere thought of the long, cold, dark winter that loomed ahead.

The night was cold. The beams in the house creaked, and once the fire had died down the icy hand of frost crept up through the floorboards. It poked its chilly fingers beneath Purdy's quilt, keeping him awake and listening to the expectant silence.

By morning, Purdy had made a decision. While Barker rekindled the fire, he scraped ice from the window and looked out at the yard where the grass was bristling with frost.

"I'm heading south," Purdy said quietly, as if testing his idea out loud.

"Did you say something?" Barker asked. The fire was ablaze in the hearth. Barker went to the kitchen to turn on the oven.

"I'm going to move away, like the birds. I'm going to follow the summer," Purdy said, louder now and more decisively. His idea had grown wings and was taking flight. "I don't like winter. I hate it."

Barker looked at Purdy for a moment as if he were speaking a foreign language. Then he shook his head and put water on to boil.

Purdy felt suddenly light. As if he really could take off and fly south with the swans. The thought of the journey made him glow with excitement.

"Come on. Let's move south for the winter and come back when the apple trees are in blossom and the swans return to their nests."

Barker sat on the other side of the table with his coffee mug. He looked at Purdy without replying.

Then he said, "We should seal up the windows today. Can you take care of that while I insulate the floorboards and put the boat in storage?"

"Weren't you even listening?" said Purdy. "I'm going away."

"Where to?" Barker asked.

"South. Where it's warm."

"It'll be warm here, once the windows and floorboards are sealed."

"It'll still be winter here."

"Of course. And after winter comes spring."

"That's when I'll come back. Just like the birds," Purdy said.

Then they were both silent.

At first Barker didn't take Purdy seriously. He had seen him get excited and then lose interest so many times, he figured this idea of going away was more of the same. While Purdy packed his bags, Barker concentrated on his work. He put the boat in storage, sealed the windows, and insulated the floor. He raked the last leaves and burned them along with twigs and scraps of timber. He did everything as usual.

Finally everything was ready: the house, the yard, and Barker were ready for winter. Purdy was ready, too. He sat on his packed bags on the porch, waiting for Barker to come in.

"What's this?" Barker asked impatiently. He was tired and hungry.

"I'm off now," Purdy said.

"Where to?"

"South."

"Silly, you don't even know which way is south."

"Of course I know. I've been watching the birds all autumn. They all fly in the same direction," Purdy said in a hurt voice, because Barker still didn't seem to be taking him seriously.

"Oh, really," Barker said. "Well then, how do you intend to get there? You don't know how to fly."

As if to answer Barker's question, Cloppity Hay clopped into the yard pulling a taxi wagon behind him.

"Cloppity's taking me to the docks," Purdy said as he heaved his bags into the wagon.

Only then did Barker start to panic.

"Are you really going? I thought you were…" He stopped mid-sentence and gulped.

"Only joking. You thought I was only joking," Purdy said with a hint of sarcasm.

"I thought it was just a phase. I didn't think you were serious," Barker tried to explain.

"I am," Purdy said and he got into the wagon.

Cloppity nodded to Barker and clopped away. Barker stood in the yard watching the wagon go out the gate and down the hill towards the village. Just before the last bend, Purdy looked back and waved. Barker returned the farewell and didn't stop waving his paw for quite some time.

Then he turned and went inside. He felt so tired, too tired even to eat or stoke the fire. So he climbed into bed and pulled the covers over his head. Barker was freezing. He shivered at the mere thought of the long, cold, dark winter ahead.

That night Barker woke to a noise. He felt a lurch of hope that it was Purdy returning, but it was only the frost making the beams creak.

All week long Barker waited for Purdy to come back.

Whenever he heard Cloppity's hooves clopping towards the driveway, he'd run outside. Or when the porch steps groaned as if someone were coming up them with a heavy bag. But Purdy didn't return. The driveway remained empty.

Barker regretted not taking his friend seriously sooner. He might have been able to talk Purdy out of it. Of course they would have made it through the winter together, just as they had every other winter. He should have realized sooner.

A week after Purdy's departure, the first snow fell. Suddenly everything was fresh and white, and Barker felt a little brighter. Not a lot, but enough to let him go out and work in the forest. All day long he chopped down trees and cut them into logs, split the logs and stacked the pieces. The day passed quickly and, when the afternoon light faded, he had to stop. As he trudged wearily home, he saw a light in the window. And he smelled smoke from the chimney.

Purdy sat reading in his armchair. When Barker came in, he looked up and smiled. Barker gulped and went to put the kettle on for tea.

They never spoke of Purdy's autumn migration. Barker never asked how far Purdy had got, whether he had spent the week in a nearby town or had sailed south as planned. Nor did Barker dare to ask why Purdy had returned, although he could guess.

However, something had changed forever. In autumn, whenever swans flew honking over the house, Barker felt terribly wistful. As if somehow something had come adrift.

BORROWERS AND LENDERS

 All afternoon the snow fell. It covered the lawn by the time Barker finally found his snow shovel under the porch. He knew all too well how it had ended up there. Purdy had been using it. Some people keep things in order and others create chaos, Barker thought as he sank the shovel into the freshly fallen snow. The most annoying thing was that the snowblower was still nowhere to be found. It would make much quicker work of clearing the snow.

Purdy had just prepared a canvas and put his tubes of oil paint out on the table when Barker came back inside. After all that hard work, Barker's fur was steaming enough to fog up the windows. On a little table by the window was an arrangement of fruit, a teapot, and Barker's bone.

"What's my bone doing in the fruit bowl?" Barker growled.

"I'm going to paint it. It's a symbol of the fleeting nature of life," Purdy said.

"Somebody around here will have a fleeting life." Barker grabbed the bone between his teeth.

"Hey! Now you've spoiled the whole thing. That bone belongs in the picture."

"And the snow shovel belongs in the shed. So does the snowblower. Besides, it's your turn to clear the snow. We agreed you'd do it this month."

"I haven't had time. I'm busy."

"So am I. But only one of us has been busy with something useful. I've been out clearing the snow."

"Art is useful too. And I didn't move the shovel or the snowblower anywhere," Purdy said defensively.

"So the snow shovel crawled under the porch by itself, did it?"

"Well, maybe I left it there by accident when I got the idea for a new painting, but I haven't touched the snowblower. You lent it to Connie Quackstrom yourself. Don't you remember?"

"No."

"Well, you did. Same with the scythe, the cake pan, the cookbook, the boat motor, and the hammock," Purdy said.

"You mean Connie Quackstrom has borrowed all those things from us?"

"Probably loads more besides, but those are the ones I remember."

"And she hasn't returned them?"

"No. Connie is known for not returning what she borrows."

Barker's face darkened. In his view, everything had its own place in the world. The scythe ought to be hung on the nail on the shed wall, the cake pan went in the cupboard on top of the cutting boards, the cookbook's place was on the shelf between B and D, there was a stand for the boat motor in the garage, and the hammock belonged between two apple trees. If you upset that order, the result was a mess, and a mess was uncomfortable. Like having your fur on the wrong way, Barker thought.

"This has to end now."

"What has to end?" Purdy asked.

"I want our things back in their proper places. We're going to have a serious talk with Connie Quackstrom."

"This I want to hear." Purdy put his paintbrush down.

"You'll hear it soon enough," Barker said.

Connie's quacking could be heard from far away as she clawed a path through the snow. Barker had invited her for afternoon tea to have a chat and tell her off about not returning their things.

"We'll be friendly but firm," Barker instructed Purdy, who merely gave an odd smile.

Barker and Purdy waited on the porch as Connie floundered through the snowdrifts towards their place. She held a pale box under her wing, which she handed to Purdy on the front steps.

"I've brought cake. I just happened to be baking when you phoned. Then I thought, why don't I take those lovely friends a proper cake we can all enjoy together."

"Thanks," Purdy said.

"That's very nice of you." Barker was pleased. "We could have baked something too, but somebody's borrowed our cake pan. Although the pan wouldn't have been much use, because somebody's borrowed our cookbook as well."

"My, look at all your snow," Connie said.

"Yes, indeed. There would be less of it if we had a snowblower, but somebody's borrowed that, too," Barker said.

"Oh, what a nuisance. That's such a shame," Connie said.

For a moment she looked really sad. As if she were remembering something she'd rather forget. For a moment she looked as if she might turn and leave. Barker felt bad about how he had behaved. So he tried to smooth things over.

"Actually, it's much better clearing the snow with a shovel. You get more exercise and a cleaner path through the snow."

"So true!" Connie said. "I noticed that your paths are neater than anyone else's in the village."

"Really?" Barker was delighted.

"Oh yes," Connie said as she followed Purdy inside.

The animals sat around the table. Purdy had cleared his painting things to one side, but the canvas was still on the easel.

"What are you painting?" Connie asked.

"A still life. It was supposed to be of a fruit bowl, a teapot, and a bone, but I might just paint the fruit bowl and the teapot," Purdy said with a glance at Barker.

"I've always said: that Purdy is so artistic. If you ask me, you deserve more recognition for your work," Connie declared as she

cut them each a slice of cake. It smelled delicious. No one said anything for a moment. Their mouths were watering at the cake.

Connie looked around the room. Her bright, kind eyes shone with approval.

"You've made it so snug in here," she said.

"You think so?" Purdy looked around as if seeing the room for the first time.

"You know, whenever I go home from here, I get a nostalgic feeling. As if I'm missing something. You don't know how much it means to me, to share friendship like this, and cake. While your paintings, Purdy, are the crowning glory. I could gaze at them all day."

Purdy looked at the table bashfully. No one had ever spoken so beautifully about his paintings.

"If only I could paint like that," Connie sighed.

"There was something we wanted to say, too," muttered Barker. He wanted to sound serious. Firm yet friendly. But it came out sounding harsh, so he regretted it at once.

"What could that be?" Connie was intrigued.

"It's about our things," Barker said grimly.

Connie waited politely for Barker to go on. But Barker remained silent. Suddenly he'd lost the nerve to press Connie for their things, when she was sitting drinking tea with them so pleasantly, not suspecting a thing.

"In my opinion, we have too many things these days. People accumulate possessions they don't even need," Connie said.

"I agree," said Purdy.

Barker was silent, but sensed that the others were waiting for his comment. "I agree," he said finally.

"Well, I should be going. It was lovely to see you both." Connie got up to go. "I'll leave the rest of the cake. You can enjoy it with a cup of tea tomorrow."

Barker went out while Connie was still chatting with Purdy about art and portraits and painting. He wished he'd been friendlier to Connie. He rushed out into the yard to clear a path, to save her waddling back through so much deep new snow. Barker tried to make an even neater path than the one Connie had praised earlier.

When Barker went back inside, Purdy was reading a book. A cheery fire was burning, and the room felt snug. Outside it had started snowing again, and Barker sat down by the fireplace to dry his fur.

"I really like your paintings, too," Barker muttered to Purdy.

"Thanks," Purdy said, moved by this surprising admission.

"And you can use my bone in your still life."

"No need," Purdy said quietly. "The thing is, I let Connie Quackstrom borrow my paints and brushes."

They were silent for a moment. The fire crackled.

"So I'll have time to clear the snow tomorrow," Purdy added.

"No need," Barker said quietly. "The thing is, I let Connie Quackstrom borrow the snow shovel too."

SUPERCAT

Purdy was bored. He was sick of everything being the same. Barker's morning tea, the taste of his porridge, the paw print on the window, the sunshine, frost crackling in the corners of the house, and wishing each other goodnight every night. It was all repeated day after day, over and over.

"How come nothing exciting ever happens?" Purdy grumbled.

"I thought I'd shovel the snow off the shed roof today," Barker said.

"What's exciting about that?"

"Nothing, but it's a nice project."

"Hmph," Purdy said. "Nobody writes adventure stories about clearing snow."

When Barker had gone, Purdy stretched out in his armchair

to read—the book was about Matilda, a girl who could move objects with the power of her mind. After a few minutes Purdy put the book down. He looked around for a suitable object and picked the vase on the windowsill. But no matter how hard Purdy stared and directed his thoughts at it, the vase wouldn't budge.

"Stupid vase. Stupid book," he sighed.

Then Purdy thought of Super Goof. Goofy the cartoon character didn't have any superpowers until he ate super goobers. Maybe Purdy's powers would only be revealed when he ate…hmm, what should he eat?

Purdy went into the pantry. There were dried mushrooms, flour, oats, cocoa powder, honey, peanuts, crackers, spices, and all the useful and useless things usually found in kitchen cupboards. Purdy took an armful of food that might give him magic powers. Then he realized that of course he couldn't be a supercat without a supercat outfit. He rummaged in his wardrobe and found a black hat, green swimming trunks, a red silk scarf, and a blue apron. He made the apron into a cape. The hat and scarf together looked very dashing, and then he put on the swimming trunks. Purdy thought for a moment, then took the food up into the attic; he didn't want Barker asking silly questions if he happened to pop in. The hatch to the attic was a tight squeeze, and the ladder was a bit rickety. As he went up and down the ladder with the food, it occurred to Purdy that Supercat would have done it in a jiffy. And Matilda would have transferred everything by thought-power.

Purdy arranged everything in neat rows on the attic floor, then examined the ingredients. He was excited about their possible effects. Would he become the Cat of Steel or Supercat, or Wonder Tom or Batcat? They all sounded equally brilliant. Barker would be astonished to see him fly out through the attic window, zoom around in the sky, then swoop down to Barker's rescue when he fell off the roof in sheer amazement and ended up dangling from the corner of the shed. Then Purdy would be a hero. Somebody would write a book about him, and somebody else would read that book and wish they could be like that, too.

Purdy started with the crackers because they tasted the best. No effect. Even after the third one, Purdy couldn't shift the old stool with the power of his mind.

Then Purdy tried the peanuts. They were what gave Super Goof his superpowers. First Purdy tried plain peanuts, then

honey roasted, then salted. Their only effect was to make him thirsty, so he drank a bottle of water. Fortunately he'd been smart enough to bring that along.

Next Purdy tried canned pineapple. It tasted so good he ate two cans. They didn't produce any new abilities either, unless you count a huge burp. Let's not count that.

Raisins didn't make Purdy fly.

Dried parsley didn't make him any stronger. Dry oats tasted terrible.

Purdy didn't even try the dried mushrooms. He wasn't that desperate to become a supercat.

After trying macaroni, cornflakes, cocoa powder (several spoonfuls), cinnamon, crackers, black pepper (fortunately there was still some water left), and strawberry jam (the last jar), Purdy gave up. He gave a deep sigh. Clearly, he was just plain Purdy, Purdy the Ordinary Cat.

He needed to lie down after his strenuous eating experiment, so he went through the hatch to reach the ladder. Or more accurately, half of Purdy went through the hatch and the other half stayed in the attic, because the hatch had shrunk significantly while he'd been up there. Purdy tried to force himself through, but only managed to get more stuck. Finally he couldn't move up or down, and he dangled there miserably in his cape and trunks, wedged in the hatch like Batcat in a trap. That's how Barker found him when he came in for a snack.

"What are you doing there?" Barker asked when he saw half of Purdy up near the ceiling.

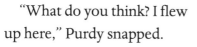

"What do you think? I flew up here," Purdy snapped.

"Do you know how to fly?" Barker asked.

"Not nearly as well as I'd like."

Barker tried hard to pull Purdy free, but couldn't. Purdy had gorged on so many goodies in the attic, his belly had doubled in size.

Finally Barker said, "We'll just have to wait until you slim down a bit."

"How long will that take?" Purdy wailed.

"Hard to say. You might be down by evening." Barker glanced at his friend's legs and smiled.

"There's one book hero you remind me of right now."

"Really?" Purdy sounded pleased.

"Yes. Vividly."

"Who do I remind you of? A superhero? Which one?" Purdy was excited.

"Winnie-the-Pooh," Barker said.

"Hmph," said Purdy.

CHRISTMAS

 As he always did on the morning of Christmas Eve, Barker brought a spruce tree inside. It was fresh and bristly and smelled wonderful. Purdy and Barker had selected it in the forest weeks before, then a few days ago Barker had brought it into the yard. Once the tree was set up inside, it was time to decorate it. Purdy had already brought the straw stars and red ornaments down from the attic, sorted the decorations and fixed any broken threads. He took it very seriously. Not a single ornament went up on the tree without careful inspection and consideration. Every so often Purdy stepped back and looked at the tree with his head on one side, then went and moved an ornament slightly to the left or right. He polished every bauble before hanging it and straightened the points on

the stars. Barker looked on with amusement but said nothing. He respected Purdy's dedication to his task. And Barker couldn't criticize, since he was just as particular when it came to the Christmas rice pudding. He measured out the milk and rice, heated them gently, stirred and tasted.

After rice pudding came a long, quiet afternoon. Barker sat by the fire and watched the flames. Purdy did a crossword. The fire crackled, the clock ticked, and everything smelled of Christmas.

For their Christmas Eve dinner they had casserole, herring salad, little pies, smoked fish, and roast marrowbones. Actually, Purdy didn't touch the marrowbones, so they tasted all the better to Barker. Purdy and Barker made pleasant small talk and avoided all topics that might lead to an argument. Christmas peace reigned in the sky-blue house on the hill.

Having eaten their fill, the two friends cleared the table and got out their domino set. They played one round, which Barker won easily. The same with the second. Usually Purdy would be agitated by now, but today he sat quietly with only a tense smile.

"Everything okay?" Barker asked gently.

"Yes," Purdy replied.

"Shall we play another round?"

"I'm not sure I have the patience," Purdy said.

Barker put the dominoes away and went to stoke the fire. Purdy squirmed in his seat.

Finally he asked, "Is it time yet?"

"Time for what? To go to bed?" Barker glanced at the clock in surprise. It was only six o'clock.

"You know what. Can't you see I'm about to burst with excitement?"

"I can see that, but I don't know why. What time is it?"

"Present time. It's time to give me my present."

Purdy's whiskers quivered. His eyes shone in the dark, and the tip of his tail flicked in circles. Barker tilted his head and looked at his friend. The longer he looked, the more agitated Purdy grew.

"But…we agreed we weren't going to exchange presents this year. We were just going to enjoy a peaceful Christmas and good food, and that's what we've been doing."

"Do you mean…you don't mean…you haven't…" Purdy couldn't finish his sentence, he was so upset as the truth began to dawn on him.

"But that's what we agreed. No presents."

"Not even a little surprise? The kind you buy even when you've agreed not to?"

"No. I didn't buy a single present. Not for you or for me."

"You can't mean that. You're just joking. Now stop it and give me my present, or I'll explode," Purdy wailed.

"I only followed our agreement. And you haven't bought me any presents, either."

"But that's different. You never expect any, but you ought to know me better. Agreeing not to buy presents meant you didn't need to buy an excessive number, but surely you bought me something? Just a tiny little thing? Maybe you hid one and forgot about it? That can happen, it's understandable," Purdy said hopefully. His voice sounded so pitiful and almost fearful,

Barker regretted that he hadn't bought even a tiny present. So he just shrugged, turned, and stoked the fire.

Purdy slumped on the bench and couldn't find a thing to say. A moment passed, then another. Silent misery had replaced the festive atmosphere. It was as if someone had opened the door and let the spirit of Christmas escape. And of course that someone was Barker. Even though he knew he'd done nothing wrong, he still felt terrible. Meanwhile, Purdy wallowed in self-pity.

Then all at once Purdy pulled himself together. He got up and went to rummage in the chest where he kept his most treasured things. Soon he returned with a pair of binoculars, an old board game, a half-finished crossword book, and a jigsaw puzzle. He placed them on the table.

"Merry Christmas, Purdy!" he said to himself. "What, for me? Gosh, that's a lot of presents. Ooh, I've always wanted a jigsaw puzzle like this. And these binoculars are very nice."

Barker watched Purdy for a moment and then went out. Soon he came back with an old sled, his best pocketknife, and a snow shovel. He put them all beneath the Christmas tree.

"Merry Christmas, Barker!" he said. "Oh, all this for me? I wasn't expecting anything. What a wonderful sled."

Purdy and Barker glanced at each other and started to giggle. Then they laughed so hard that the Christmas spirit peeped around the edge of the door then flooded back in, as Purdy and Barker gave each other a big hug.

"You know what? You can have my binoculars for your present." Purdy placed them around Barker's neck. Barker couldn't say a thing, he was so touched. He had always secretly admired Purdy's binoculars.

"You need them more than I do," Purdy said.

"And you can have my sled," Barker said.

"Oh, you shouldn't," Purdy protested.

"You can have it."

Purdy couldn't contain his joy. A sled was what he had secretly wanted most of all for Christmas. One just like Barker's.

"Of course, what I meant was, you can have the binoculars almost all for yourself," Purdy remarked.

WINTER SPORTS

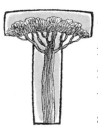"This is a beautiful morning," Barker announced from the doorway. Purdy was curled up by the fire with only his whiskers and yellow eyes visible. He glared at Barker, who had clumps of snow in his fur and frost on his whiskers.

"What are you doing lolling about there?" Barker asked.

Purdy was indignant. "Lolling? I'm doing my best to avoid freezing to death."

"Nonsense. The weather's perfect out there."

"For snowmen and polar bears maybe, but I am a very sensitive, sophisticated being."

"You may well be, but anyway, your skis are ready. I've varnished and waxed them."

Purdy stared as if he'd been given terrible news. Or seen a monster under the bed. Or got a bone for his birthday. Or...

"Skis?" he barely managed to whisper.

"Yes. Don't you remember, you promised to come skiing with me?"

"No," Purdy said.

"You said if I built a gazebo for you to sit and admire sunsets and paint pictures in, you'd come skiing with me."

"Next year," said Purdy, his voice croaky with shock. "I mean, I'll go with you next year. Definitely. Next winter is forecast to be a lot warmer."

"That's what you said last year." Barker sounded very disappointed.

"Did I really?"

"And the year before. And the year before that. That gazebo is so old now, it needs a new roof."

"Well, let's agree you'll fix the roof and then I'll go skiing with you." Purdy pulled the quilt tighter around himself.

"I don't agree," Barker sighed. His ears and tail drooped, and his whole body slumped, as if his backbone had melted in the warm room.

"Wait," Purdy said, as Barker turned to take Purdy's skis back to the shed to store for next winter, and the next and the next after that. "I was only joking. Sure, I'll come."

Barker had everything set to go. The skis were waxed, the sandwiches were packed and he had skied the trail several times in recent days. Sunlight sparkled on the snow. Purdy didn't need to do anything except put on his skis and enjoy it.

"My skis are too short," he said.

"They're the same length as before," Barker assured him.

"The poles are too short."

"They're the same length as before."

"The bindings are too tight."

"They're the same as before."

"The sun's too bright."

"That's the same as before, too."

"This is just awful. It's no use."

"Same as before," Barker sighed and slowly set off along the ski trail. Purdy watched helplessly for a moment, then followed. They crossed the vegetable garden and turned between the mushroony shed and the crabbage enclosure to go down the hill towards the lake. Barker went first. He tucked his poles under his arms, crouched and took off, zooming down the hill. Then it was Purdy's turn. He spread his arms wide, flailed with his poles, kept his legs straight, and wobbled down, shrieking all the way. Barker was afraid Purdy would fall, which would mean the end of their outing but, wonder of wonders, Purdy made it down in one piece.

"You did fine," Barker exclaimed.

"It was terrible," Purdy said. "I want to do it again, but better."

Because Purdy couldn't climb back to the top of the hill under his own steam, Barker had to drag him. Then they went down again—Barker smoothly, Purdy wobbling and shrieking.

"Great. That was much better," Barker praised him.

"You're just saying that so you don't have to help me up again."

"Not at all. Sure, I'll help you if you want. But maybe we'd better continue on our way."

"I knew you didn't want to."

And so Barker had no choice but to drag Purdy up the hill for a third attempt, in case he thought Barker didn't want to. Finally Purdy was happy with the way he skied down, which was just as wobbly and shrieky as the previous times but at least they could go on their way. And a good thing, too, because Barker couldn't have dragged his friend up the hill one more time.

"Too much glare," Purdy complained beside the lake. "It hurts my sensitive eyes."

"It is very bright. I'm sorry I forgot to pack your sunglasses," Barker said.

"I always have to think of everything," Purdy said as Barker handed him his own sunglasses.

And so they carried on. Quite slowly, since Barker had to squint as he skied because the sun's glare hurt his sensitive eyes.

Fortunately in the shade of the trees on the other side of the lake the snow was less dazzling. Barker skied doggedly to the end of a peninsula where the day before he had prepared a campsite. The snow had been trodden down, the firewood was ready, and Barker had even cut down a tree so they would have a nice dry trunk to sit on as they ate their sandwiches by the campfire.

"What are you doing?" Purdy asked in horror as Barker took off his backpack to start the campfire.

"Don't you want something to eat? I've got hot chocolate and fish sandwiches."

"Yes, but not here."

"Why not?"

"The sun isn't even shining properly here. Plus, the scenery's much nicer on the other side." Purdy pointed a shaky paw to where he wanted to set up camp.

"All right. Wait here. I'll go and make a campsite over there," Barker sighed, taking his hatchet from his backpack.

"Here? I'll be frozen to the bone and catch a cold and then the whole trip will be ruined," Purdy whined. But he calmed down when Barker lit the campfire and poured him a cup of hot chocolate.

Barker trudged through heavy snow to the other side of the peninsula. He stamped the snow down and broke off dead twigs for a fire. He chopped down a tree and lopped off its branches, then cut its trunk in two and dragged them to the campfire for seats. When everything was finally ready, Barker straightened his aching back and looked around. Purdy had been right: this spot was much prettier. The sun was shining, and Barker was starving after all that effort. On his way back he took care to make a nice trail so Purdy would have no trouble reaching their new campsite. Barker could hardly wait for their tasty lunch. That was always the best part of an outing, he thought. Besides, he was sure that once they were sitting by the campfire munching on Barker's delicious fish sandwiches, Purdy would agree that the ski trip had been a brilliant idea.

"You took your time," Purdy said when Barker turned up grinning. "I was starting to freeze. That campfire of yours was none too big," he grumped.

Barker glanced at the logs beside the fire, which he had piled up the day before. Purdy hadn't added a single one to the fire. But Barker didn't say anything as he put on his backpack. It felt strangely light.

"And there weren't many fish sandwiches either." Purdy wiped crumbs from his whiskers. "And the hot chocolate was on the lukewarm side."

Barker stopped in his tracks and stared ahead without seeing. He came to the painful conclusion that Purdy had eaten all their packed lunch while he was working hard on their new campsite.

"Are we going now? I'm getting chilly," Purdy said, jumping up. He put on his skis and flew back the way they had come.

Worn out, Barker turned his skis around. He was hungry and tired, and couldn't keep up with Purdy, who dashed across the ice then up their hill as nimbly as a young deer.

Purdy was already waiting cheerfully in the yard when Barker finally made it home.

"That was a lovely outing," Purdy said. "Let's do it again tomorrow."

A SINGING CONTEST

Purdy was singing. He stood in the middle of the room and warmed up with a low *ma-me-mi-mo-mu, ma-me-mi-mo*. Then he sang higher: *ha-ha-ha-ha-ha-ha-haaa*. And then *noo-noo-noo-noo-noo-noo-noo-noooo*, high and low. It wasn't even six o'clock in the morning.

Barker had already tried putting a pillow over his ears, but that didn't help one bit. Purdy's voice was loud but, sadly, not beautiful. Especially if you asked Barker at 5:30 a.m.

Barker sighed, got up and went to put on the kettle. Purdy's eyes were screwed shut and he sang with all his might. This had been going on for two weeks, ever since Purdy had innocently asked Barker, "Do you think I can sing?"

"Oh, sure," Barker had replied.

"But do I have a nice voice?"

"Sure," Barker had said, not suspecting what it would lead to.

Now he regretted it. Since then Purdy had been getting up at the crack of dawn to do vocal exercises that usually lasted all day. Purdy certainly could be lazy and comfort-loving but, when he badly wanted to do something, he could also be very determined. Now Purdy wanted to sing.

Barker went to sit on the porch with his tea. The sun rose from behind a veil of mist, the birds were chirping, and the first bumblebees were out. It would have been a lovely spring morning if not for the cat's yowling accompaniment.

Barker went over to the garden swing. From there Purdy's singing was less distinct. If you didn't know, you might think it was a jet passing overhead or a far-off thunderstorm. Steam rose from Barker's mug of tea. The breeze carried a light scent of fresh soil, which to Barker was the nicest smell on earth. He shut his eyes and sniffed. His thoughts floated happily into the sky, where white sheep-clouds frolicked and there was lovely silence.

Barker's daydream was broken by a dreadful screech. For a moment he thought the swing had collapsed or the whole hill had split open, but it was only Purdy, who had come outside to sing.

Purdy stopped and asked, "What do you think?"

"Fine," Barker said unenthusiastically.

"You sound like you didn't really enjoy it."

"Oh, I did. You have a gorgeous voice."

"You're just flattering me."

"Not at all."

"All right. I believe you. Do you think I should enter the village singing contest?"

Barker wondered what to say. He knew the annual contest was coming up, and Purdy obviously had no chance of winning. The judge's comments might hurt his feelings, and of course Barker didn't want that to happen. Then again, if nobody told Purdy his singing was ear-splittingly painful, Barker would be forced to listen to it for who knew how long—maybe all summer. It would be much better if someone else critiqued Purdy's singing. That way Barker could avoid an awkward situation.

"Definitely. In fact, I insist you enter," Barker told him.

That made Purdy so happy, he sang "The Black Cat Tango" and "Life in the Trenches" to Barker right there. Barker sat and listened to both songs with a patient expression on his face.

Two days before the contest, Henny Cluckington came to visit. Purdy was inside singing while Barker sat outside wearing safety ear protectors and reading the newspaper.

"Is someone using a circular saw nearby?" Henny asked.

"Huh?" Barker uncovered his ears.

"That awful racket. It's like being in a sawmill."

"Purdy's singing. He's rehearsing for the contest."

"I see. In that case, should they impose an age restriction? Children might be frightened."

"I'd be more worried about the judge's mental health," Barker said.

"Ah, I was meaning to remind you about that." Henny gave Barker a strange look.

"The judge's mental health?" Barker asked. "What's that got to do with me?"

"You're the judge. Don't you remember? It's your turn."

Slowly Barker put his paper down. As he looked at Henny, his eyes glazed over and his head started whirling with a thousand things, like a machine whose cogs had all come loose at once. Gradually it came back to him. The singing contest was held every year, with a different judge each time. Everyone in the village took their turn. This year Barker was to be the judge.

"I can't do it," Barker blurted.

"What do you mean?" Henny asked.

"Purdy's a contestant, so I can't be the judge. I'd definitely be biased."

"But everybody knows each other around here. No matter who the judge is, they're bound to have friends among the competitors."

"Let's swap our turns. Couldn't you do it this time, and I'll do it next year?" Barker pleaded.

"That won't work. I'm taking part in the contest myself this year. And from the sound of things, I won't come last." Henny glanced towards the house, where Purdy was currently exceeding the sound barrier.

It was no use. When the day of the contest arrived and the entire village had gathered in the hall for the singing contest, the judge sat down behind his table: a miserable-looking dog with drooping ears. He recalled his conversation with Purdy at breakfast that morning, when he had informed Purdy of his duty.

"That doesn't matter," Purdy had said. "You'll be fair and honest."

"Is that what you think?" Barker was delighted.

"Sure. But you won't need to be unnecessarily harsh with the others. Everybody will be able to hear how much better I am," Purdy said, and Barker's optimism vanished as quickly as it had appeared.

Barker shuddered. He briefly considered fleeing, but the first contestant was already coming onstage, and the densely packed audience meant there was no chance of escape. Barker was stuck. He would have to take whatever might come.

First up was Winky Pig. She performed "This Little Piggy Went to Market," as she did every year.

Barker gave his verdict: "Very much a personal interpretation. Especially the part where you sang 'Wee wee weeeeee'—that sounded very authentic."

Next to sing was Martha Woollaston. She sang a Swedish number entitled "Bää Bää, White Sheep."

"Lovely rendition. Especially when you sang 'Bää bää'—that sounded very authentic," Barker told her.

"Lovely rendition. Especially the part where you sang 'Neigh-nonny-nonny'—that was very authentic-sounding," Barker told Cloppity Hay, who sang "Sigh No More, Ladies."

"Lovely rendition. Especially 'With a moo-moo here and a moo-moo there'—most impressive," he told Daisy Butterfield.

And so on and so forth, until there was only one contestant to go: Purdy.

Purdy stepped onto the stage and planted his feet wide. He looked out over the audience and took a deep breath. Barker broke into a cold sweat. He wished for a miracle. He desperately hoped that sweet sounds would suddenly spill from Purdy's mouth and enchant everyone. But miracles are rare, and Purdy's first screech shattered the plasterwork on the walls, made the little ones cry, and sent the entire audience charging for the exit. Purdy knew nothing of this, because he was singing his heart out with his eyes shut tight. Yowling, howling, shrieking, and screeching as never before.

When Purdy finished, Barker was the only one left in the hall. Having heard it so often, he was the only one who could listen to Purdy's performance all the way through.

Purdy opened his eyes and saw the empty hall.

"Where is everybody?" he asked in surprise.

"Outside."

"But why? I was singing."

"That's why," Barker said. "It was horrible."

Gradually the audience returned to the hall and Barker declared Winky the winner of the contest. After the prizes were handed out, he looked for Purdy but couldn't find him among the crowd.

Purdy was sitting on the garden swing when Barker got home, out of breath. He had run all the way. He sat down beside Purdy and said nothing. The evening sky was dark. Somewhere

someone was whistling faintly. Barker didn't know what to say. He was afraid he'd hurt his friend's feelings so badly Purdy might never get over it. But there was nothing else he could have done. He had decided for once to be honest.

After a long pause, Purdy said, "At first I was furious, but now I understand why you said that."

"You do?"

"Sure. You couldn't let me win, because that would have led to complaints. I'm your best friend. Right?"

"Right," Barker said. "You're my best friend." Which was the truth.

"Next year somebody else will be the judge. Then I'll win every prize going. I'm thinking of singing 'Papa's Got a Brand New Bag,' accompanying myself on the bagpipes," Purdy said with a dreamy look.

Barker sighed, but very softly so Purdy wouldn't hear.

PERFECT

 Out of the blue one day, Purdy asked, "Do you think I'm perfect?"

Barker was mowing the lawn. He glanced sideways at his friend, who was eagerly awaiting his answer. "Well, nobody's absolutely perfect," Barker said.

"But am I?"

Barker's thoughts raced. The memory of Purdy's excitement about singing after he had complimented his voice was fresh in his mind. If Barker now told him he was perfect, who knew what the consequences might be? On the other hand, if he told him he wasn't, the consequences might be worse. A butterfly fluttered among the flowers. It was bright and beautiful. It gave Barker an idea.

"Look at this butterfly. Do you think it's perfect?" he asked.

"It's a perfect butterfly," Purdy said.

"There you are. And you are a perfect Purdy." He was pleased to have come up with that clever response.

"A perfect Purdy," Purdy sighed as he walked off.

Barker carried on mowing the lawn, humming a tune. In his opinion, he was a perfect genius.

Purdy and Barker had planned to go shopping at the market that afternoon. Barker wanted a new firewood carrier and Purdy was going to buy some wool from Martha Woollaston.

Barker was already waiting impatiently in the yard, but there was no sign of Purdy. Finally Barker lost his patience and went inside, where he found Purdy sitting on the edge of his bed.

"Why are you dawdling? The market won't be open much longer."

"I can't go," Purdy said miserably.

"Why not? We've been talking about going for over a week."

"Everybody will laugh at me."

"Why on earth would they laugh at you?"

"If I mess up. Everybody will laugh if I stumble or say 'wood blarn' when I mean wool yarn, or if I get sweaty while I'm shopping."

Barker had no idea what Purdy was talking about.

"We all make mistakes sometimes," Barker said. "There's no harm in that."

"Yes, there is. If I mess up, I won't be perfect any more," Purdy wailed.

Suddenly Barker knew what was the matter. Poor Purdy thought he wasn't allowed to make any mistakes. And that was more than anyone could bear.

"What if I happen to meet Henny or somebody and we chat about the weather. Then I say what a cloudy day it is and Henny says it's actually been sunny."

"So what?" Barker asked.

"Henny will think I'm stupid if I say it's cloudy when it's sunny. And she'll think so even more when she sees I've bought knitting wool on a hot, sunny day. Or what if I put on my nice black hat then find that nobody else in the whole market square is wearing one, because it's far too hot outside. Everybody will give me strange looks and laugh behind my back."

"So what?"

"How in the world can I be perfect if the whole village thinks I'm stupid?" Purdy moaned, hanging his head.

Now Barker really started to worry. He could see that "So what" wasn't enough to console Purdy. Barker racked his brain for a way to help Purdy understand that "a perfect Purdy" didn't mean he shouldn't make mistakes—quite the opposite. Purdy was perfectly himself, mistakes and all.

"Watch," Barker said. He went over to the hat rack, picked the most hideous old hat and put it on. "What do I look like now?"

"Like Barker," Purdy said.

Then Barker dug his ski boots out of the closet and sat down to put them on.

"What are you doing?" Purdy asked.

"I thought I'd ski to the market."

"But the snow's all gone," Purdy said.

"So what?" Barker went out to the shed to fetch his skis.

Purdy stood on the porch and watched in disbelief as Barker scooted across the lawn towards the gate and then trudged down the hill towards the village and the market.

"You're crazy. Everybody will laugh at you," Purdy shouted after him.

"So what!" Barker shouted back.

Just then, a butterfly landed on the porch railing. Purdy recognized it as the one they had seen that morning. Now, though, he noticed that it had a tiny piece of wing missing. It was still beautiful, though. A perfect butterfly.

Purdy ran to the shed for the kick-sled. He wanted to make it to the market in time.

TREASURE

 A treasure map turned up during the spring-cleaning. It was in an old chest in the attic—just the sort of place you'd expect to find one. It was on old, torn, and yellowed paper, with a compass rose printed in the bottom left corner and an X in the middle, just as there should be. And so there could be no mistaking it, across the top in big letters were the words "TREASURE MAP."

"This chest belonged to my great-great-grandfather," Barker said. "He was the mascot on board Captain Cookbook's ship."

"Was he the one with a hook for a hand?" Purdy asked.

"That was Captain Hook. Captain Cookbook was his brother. Legend has it that he liked to boil his enemies' bones for soup."

Purdy and Barker studied the map. Besides the compass directions and the X, it showed a few trees and a house.

"Do you think this is a real treasure map?" Purdy's voice was trembling.

"Could be. My great-great-grandfather was a pirate's dog."

"Is the house on this map our house?"

"Probably."

"Are we going to search for the treasure?"

"Maybe. We'll have to think about it."

To Purdy's amazement, Barker rolled the document up and put it back in the chest. Then they went downstairs, where Barker put on the kettle.

Purdy was antsy. He simply couldn't understand why they weren't out digging already. Even worse, Barker sat calmly slurping his tea.

"What kind of treasure could it be?" Purdy asked.

"Who knows?"

"How did your great-great-grandfather end up with this place, anyway?"

"Maybe he was given it as a reward for bravery. Or maybe he deserted the ship and took some of the pirates' booty with him."

"Why aren't we going out to dig now?"

"Because we don't know."

"Know what?"

"What kind of treasure it is. Sometimes treasures only cause trouble."

"Nonsense. Treasure makes the people who find it rich and happy."

Barker said nothing, just blew on his tea and looked outside. Purdy squirmed in his seat and finally could stand it no longer. He went outside to search for signs of treasure in the yard.

That afternoon Barker took the map from the chest. He measured the yard carefully, counting his steps from the side of the house to the trees. He checked and measured and finally stopped in the middle of the vegetable garden that was bordered by raspberry bushes.

"Around here," Barker said.

"Around here or exactly here?" Purdy asked impatiently.

"Here," Barker said.

In a flash Purdy fetched a spade and started to dig. Dirt flew up. In the soft soil, the hole quickly deepened. When his enthusiasm faded, Purdy took a break.

"First I'm going to buy a new car," he mused, sitting on the edge of the hole. "I'll drive it through the village and everyone will envy me because I'm so rich and happy."

Then he dug some more but soon stopped again, lost in another daydream. "Or maybe I'll buy a plane."

"You need an airport for a plane," Barker pointed out.

"We can fill in that stupid lake and build an airport there."

And then Purdy dug some more.

Barker sat down by the raspberry bushes to watch as Purdy gradually disappeared from view. Luckily it was still early spring so Barker hadn't planted the carrots or potatoes yet, otherwise they would have ended up in bad shape.

"Phew," Purdy said from the depths of the hole.

"Looks like hard work," Barker said.

"I don't mind. It just occurred to me, what if the treasure's so small there's not enough for a plane and an airport?"

"Then you simply buy one or the other."

"But what will I do with a plane but no airport, or an airport with no plane?" Purdy moaned.

"Buy the car instead."

"What, only a car? One lousy car?" Purdy's head appeared above the hole. He looked indignant. "Do you mean to say I should settle for some old rust-bucket, when other people who find treasure get to buy planes and airports and probably rocket launch pads as well?"

"No, I didn't say that. You're the one who brought up the car and the plane."

"What would I do with a car? I don't even know how to drive."

Purdy climbed up out of the hole and stood in front of Barker. "I have a feeling your great-great-grandfather wasn't even a pirate," he said.

"No, he wasn't a pirate. He was a ship's mascot dog, if you remember what I said."

"And I bet that Captain Cookbook was a bungling amateur, whose treasure couldn't even buy a bicycle."

"Maybe. They say he was so fierce he sank his enemies' ships before he had time to rob them."

"Anyway, I've already got a bike, which is still at the bottom of the lake." Purdy threw his spade to the ground and ran inside.

Barker calmly got up and wandered over to the edge of the hole. It was deep and wide. And on the far side he could make out something with sharp edges. It might be a rock or…

Barker took the spade and started throwing the dirt back into the hole. He hummed softly to himself. The carrots would be nice and big and juicy this year, since the soil had been properly loosened for once.

HAVING FUN

Barker leaned on the table and watched Purdy leaping around the room after a fly. He wasn't really trying to catch it, just shooing it off wherever it landed.

"I envy you," Barker told him. "You know how to have fun. I don't."

"Aren't you having fun right now?"

"No." There was a note of sadness in Barker's voice.

"Why not?"

"I'm thinking about the garden furniture I should paint today. Then I should shift the compost heap and fill the potholes in the driveway."

"I've got an idea," Purdy said. "Forget all those boring chores. Let's have a party. A surprise party!"

"A surprise party. Yes, that would be fun!" Barker agreed.

Purdy loved celebrations, especially surprise parties. That's when somebody thinks they're in for an ordinary evening at home, drinking tea and going to bed early so they can get up bright and early the next morning, then suddenly they find themselves in a cheerful crowd who are all cracking old jokes and making new friends. To Purdy, surprise parties were the best thing in the world.

While Purdy fetched a box of silly hats from the attic and tried them on in the mirror, Barker drew up a menu, guest list, shopping list, and to-do list.

While Purdy laughed as he cut tissue paper into funny decorations and wrote invitations with goofy verses on them, Barker picked carrots and lettuce from the garden, went to the store, put the food on to cook, and painted the garden furniture.

While Purdy came up with silly party games and clowned around the yard in a top hat and thick glasses, Barker went to shift the compost heap, filled the potholes in the driveway, and made a big batch of juice for the party.

"Isn't this fun?" Purdy tooted on a little plastic horn.

"Not yet. I still have to set the table and fold the napkins."

"But isn't it nice we're having a surprise party?"

"Work first, then fun," Barker said.

Purdy looked at his friend with concern. Barker was tired and dusty from his day's work.

"You've got the wrong attitude," Purdy said.

"That may be, but with your attitude we'd be sitting in the garden swing right now in silly hats, tooting horns. The driveway

would still have potholes, the compost heap wouldn't have been shifted, and the garden furniture would still need a coat of paint."

"Perhaps, but we'd both be having fun."

"No, I'd still be thinking the whole time about the driveway, the garden furniture, and the compost." Barker's tail drooped.

Purdy took his friend by the shoulders and made him sit down. He put his top hat and funny glasses on Barker.

"Now you're going to have fun, and I'll take care of the rest of the work," he said.

Purdy folded the napkins and put them beside the plates.

"That's not the way I fold them," Barker pointed out.

"Be quiet and have fun," Purdy said.

Purdy chucked a handful of black pepper and a couple of pinches of salt into the stew.

"I usually measure the seasonings with a spoon," Barker said.

"Why don't you go outside and have a nice roll in the yard?" Purdy suggested.

Purdy mopped the floor. He did a few ballet steps with the mop, then pretended to be a famous ice hockey player.

"You missed a spot in that corner," Barker said.

"Why don't you have a nap so you can stay awake for the party?"

"I can't sleep when I'm this worried."

"What are you worried about?"

"This party. Is it going to be a success? Will everybody have a nice time? Will the food be good? Will the guests enjoy themselves? Will anybody even turn up?"

"But a surprise can't fail. Nobody expects anything, because it's a surprise party."

Barker thought for a moment, but couldn't find anything else to say. He got up and went out.

That evening the yard filled with guests. Everyone was pleasantly surprised and delighted with the invitation. Daisy Butterfield told a joke about a cow and a fireman. Everybody had heard it a hundred times before, but they still laughed. Connie Quackstrom and Winky Pig did the Birdy Song dance. Everybody had seen it a thousand times before, but they still laughed. Henny recited a funny verse she had written. Everybody had heard it a million times already, but still they clapped.

Barker was the only one who didn't clap or laugh. He sat in the garden swing and watched the guests, who praised the food and admired the freshly painted garden furniture and the smooth driveway. Then he fell asleep. He was obviously having a lovely dream because he looked very happy. As if he was having a whole lot of fun.

LIKE CAT AND DOG

Who's smarter: a cat or a dog? On that question, Purdy and Barker occasionally argued, although for the most part they lived peaceably in their little house on a hill where the forest meets the sky.

Their arguments usually broke out all of a sudden, for no particular reason. It might be Barker accidentally dropping his mug of tea, which prompted a comment from Purdy. "Cats are careful. Refined and elegant, and they never drop anything." Or Purdy would happen to mislay his book, which Barker could find just by sniffing the air. "Dogs have an exceptional sense of smell. They're precise and practical and never lose a thing."

Other times they would argue whether cats were more flexible, cuter, furrier, more independent, and mysterious than dogs, or whether dogs were more faithful, kind-hearted, braver, cuter, furrier, and stronger than cats. They never settled the matter.

Purdy was searching in the yard for his book about plants. He was sure he'd left it by the flowerbed the day before when he was trying to identify and record all the plants in the garden.

"Did you move my book?" he asked Barker, who was watering the sunflowers in a wide-brimmed straw hat.

"Why would I do that? I don't need a book to know what the plants are."

"Is that so? In that case, what's a *Taraxacum officinale*?"

"Never heard of it."

"It's a dandelion."

"And dandelion's a dandy name for it, so that's what I use," Barker muttered.

"What about the Latin name? You can't claim to know about plants if you don't know their scientific names."

"By the way, you're standing in the stinging nettle," Barker said. "I don't know its scientific name."

"Yeeow!" Purdy yelped, leaping straight up. Then he dashed inside to put cream on his nettle rash.

One day Henny Cluckington came up the lane. She was out of breath from climbing the steep hill, so she sat in the shade of a birch tree and gratefully accepted the glass of juice Barker brought out to her. Purdy left his plant collection and came over to sit with Barker and Henny.

"Did you know Daisy Butterfield has bought a ball?" Henny began. "It's not my place to say a cow shouldn't be an athlete, but still. The whole village has gone without milk while the only cow stands in the field with her ball, waiting for someone to come and give her a game."

"Daisy's good at waiting. Cows are very patient," Barker said.

"But they're not very smart," Purdy added.

"Unlike chickens. We're known for our intelligence," Henny said proudly.

"Yes, we know what they say about birds' brains," Purdy said.

"They're famous," Barker agreed.

"Really? Well, anyway, I came up here to ask if you'd go and talk some sense into Daisy. I'm sure she'd listen to you."

"What should we tell her?" Barker asked.

"To end this nonsense and give us some milk," Henny huffed.

So Purdy and Barker had no choice but to go along with Henny and speak to Daisy.

The situation was exactly as Henny had described. Daisy stood in the field, staring at a white ball with her big moist eyes. She chewed pensively, but was otherwise motionless. Several villagers, including Winky Pig and Cloppity Hay, had gathered at the edge of the field with their milk cans and buckets. When Purdy and Barker arrived, they were all standing around looking helpless.

"It's good you're here. We've asked Daisy to take a quick break from staring and give us some milk, but she won't listen, and sees nothing but the ball," Winky explained.

"What if somebody took the ball and hid it? Just for a minute or two," Purdy suggested.

"She'd put her horns into you." Cloppity pointed to his bucket, which had a hole in the side.

"She'd kick you." Winky pointed out the big dent in her milk can.

"Oh," Purdy said.

Purdy looked at the cow and the ball, then turned to Barker.

"Barker, shall we agree that whoever gets a bucketful of milk from Daisy is the smarter one?"

Barker glanced at Purdy. Of course he suspected monkey business, but could find no reason to object. "All right. And then we'll never have to argue about it again."

"It's a deal. And here are our witnesses."

"Deal."

Purdy and Barker shook paws, which marked the start of the contest to decide once and for all whether a cat is smarter than a dog or vice versa.

Henny tossed a coin to see who would go first. Barker won.

"This will be quick," Barker said confidently as Winky handed him a bucket.

"Watch out for the horns," Cloppity said.

"Watch out for the hooves," Winky added.

Barker went straight over to Daisy. He trotted right up, put down the bucket and greeted her.

"Hello, Daisy. What a nice ball you have there."

"Hello," Daisy replied warily.

"So, what are you doing?"

"Waiting," Daisy whispered.

"Waiting for what?"

"For it to hatch," Daisy said solemnly.

"I see." Barker scratched his ear. The situation was more complicated than he had expected. Daisy clearly thought the ball was some kind of egg. Barker, on the other hand, understood balls well enough to know it would be quite a while before anything hatched from it.

"What's it going to be?" Barker asked.

"How should I know? I'm not the one who laid it. Cows don't lay eggs," Daisy snapped.

"I'm no expert on hatching eggs either, but don't they need to be sat on?"

"Do you think so?" Daisy asked.

"Yes. That's what it takes. I could sit on it for a bit while you fill up this bucket with milk." With this kind of cunning Barker was bound to be the winner.

Daisy looked at the ball and then at Barker. "Thanks, but I'll sit on it myself." She lowered herself onto the ball, which disappeared beneath cow and udder.

"What about the milk?" Barker asked in desperation.

"I'll give it some milk once it's hatched," Daisy said.

Barker could only admit defeat and trudge back to the others.

"Here, you try." Barker handed the bucket to Purdy.

"This is almost too easy," Purdy laughed to himself. Daisy eyed him suspiciously as he crept towards her.

"Keep your distance," Daisy warned.

"Here, let me help you," Purdy said.

"No way. I can handle this myself."

"But you're doing it all wrong."

"How?"

"You don't sit on it."

"But Barker said I had to."

"Pfft, Barker's a dog. What does he know? You should have asked me from the start. I'm an expert."

Daisy sized Purdy up, then slowly got up off the ball.

"Then show me—but don't harm it."

"Of course not. I'm famous for my velvet touch," Purdy said. He grabbed the ball and started tossing it around.

"What are you doing? Be careful!"

"Don't worry. Watch this." Purdy switched paws. He spun the ball on one paw, threw it high, trapped it with his chest, gave it a kick and headed it.

Daisy looked on in horror.

Then Purdy said, "Now it's your turn. I'll throw the ball and you head it to me."

"Are you sure this is the right thing to do?"

"Sure. I'll teach you everything I know, and all I ask in return is a bucketful of milk," Purdy promised.

"All right."

"Good. Now I'll throw the ball, and you head it back. Ready?"

Daisy nodded and waited. Purdy threw the ball high in the air. Daisy followed its arc and then tossed her head. There was a faint thunk as the ball hit one of Daisy's horns, was punctured, and stuck there.

"What happened to the egg?" she asked. She couldn't see it.

"Egg? What egg?" Purdy asked.

"The one you threw. Has it hatched already?"

Purdy looked in dismay at the deflated ball on Daisy's horn. Of course he couldn't say anything.

"What about the milk?" Purdy asked desperately.

"First I'm going to look for the egg." Daisy wandered away over the field.

"I guess it was a tie," Barker concluded as they trudged back home.

"But I got closer," Purdy boasted.

"If I were you, I wouldn't want to be at all close when Daisy figures out where her egg ended up."

And there they were, arguing again about whether a dog is smarter than a cat or vice versa. They never did manage to settle the matter.

DO YOU DARE?

Barker believed that hard work pays off. He also believed that all's well that ends well; a bird in the hand is worth two in the bush; if you set a trap for others, you'll fall into it yourself; the early bird catches the worm; and a hidden bone is the best bone. He'd come up with that last proverb himself.

Purdy believed that if you wish for something hard enough, it will come true. Purdy wished he could fly. Every morning when he woke, he lay there a moment, checking whether wings had grown overnight or if that was just a corner of the quilt against his back. Then he would creep up to the mirror, slowly turn and look over his shoulder—if cats have shoulders—to see if there was any kind of bulge where a wing would soon sprout, like a wisdom tooth.

"That's silly. Have you ever heard of a cat with wings?" Barker snorted.

"No," Purdy admitted, "but that doesn't mean I won't be the first."

"It's still silly." Barker remembered all too well Purdy trying to ride his bicycle to the moon. And the time Purdy had headed south with the migrating birds, and how lonely he had felt with Purdy gone.

"Maybe tomorrow," Purdy said, and went outside.

"Hopefully never," Barker said under his breath.

Days passed, and no wings sprouted. But Purdy wasn't discouraged.

"Maybe tomorrow," he said, and then his mind wandered elsewhere.

Barker, on the other hand, couldn't stop thinking of wings. He even had dreams where Purdy woke with huge brown wings on his back. He spread them out like a newly hatched butterfly, then soared into the sky. Barker heard the heavy beat of wings as Purdy rose higher and higher, until he joined a V of cranes and they all vanished over the horizon. Then Barker woke up, drenched in sweat and gasping for breath.

One such night Barker made a decision. If Purdy ever did grow wings, he would be prepared. He wouldn't let his friend fly away on his own. He would go with him.

The next morning Barker watched closely as Purdy once again checked in the mirror, shrugged, and said maybe his wings

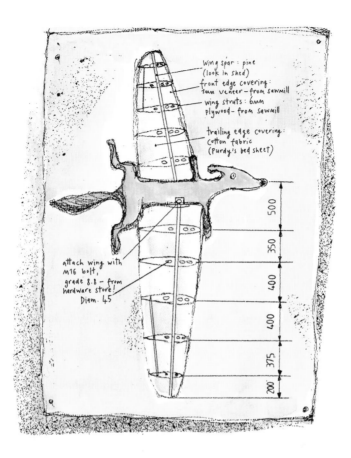

would sprout the next day. When he'd gone out, Barker sneaked over to his workshop, closed the door firmly, took out a sketchbook, compass, and ruler, and got down to work.

Barker didn't believe in miracles, at least not for himself. Although he was afraid that Purdy would wake up one day with wings, he didn't believe it would happen to him. Barker was more of a practical dog, so he had decided to build his own wings. Then if by some miracle Purdy became a winged cat, he'd slip on his own pair and follow him to the ends of the earth.

"A cat with wings! Who ever heard of such a thing?" Barker snorted as he opened his sketchbook and began drawing a diagram of a winged dog.

Barker hid away all week in the workshop. At first Purdy didn't notice anything unusual. Barker was always busy with something: assembling a greenhouse, chopping firewood, or putting up a clothesline. Barker had always taken care of the housework as well. He just loved cooking and cleaning. Yes, it's apparently possible to love those things.

On Tuesday dinner was nearly an hour late. On Wednesday the casserole was burnt. Dinner on Thursday was leftover burnt casserole from the day before. On Friday dust balls were building up in the corners and Barker didn't make any dinner at all. That's when Purdy started to worry. He went out to the workshop to find Barker, but the door was locked. Purdy frowned. The workshop door was never locked.

"Yoo-hoo," he shouted through the door. It was silent inside. "Barker, are you in there?" Still no answer. "I know you're in there. What are you up to?"

"I'm… reading," came Barker's reply. He sounded cagey.

"How come the door's locked?"

"I want to read in peace and quiet."

"So, what are you reading?"

"It's a secret."

Purdy was shocked. His friend, the dog who hardly read at all, had locked himself in the workshop to read a secret book, neglecting all his usual work. Then again, Purdy loved reading, so he knew that a book could be so exciting it had to be read in peace and quiet. He was actually pleased in a way that Barker was finally interested in reading. Maybe he'd get to read the book when Barker had finished, and they could talk about it together by the fire in the evening.

"All right," Purdy said. "Enjoy your reading."

After a week or so, Barker was finished. He locked the workshop door carefully, brushed the dust from his fur, and went back to his regular jobs. His mind was easier now, because he knew that if Purdy flew off one day, he could follow wherever he went.

It never hurts to be prepared, Barker thought.

That would have been the end of it if Purdy hadn't been so curious and persistent. Purdy's wings would have stayed in his dreams, and Barker's up in the workshop rafters. But that book was bugging Purdy—the book Barker had read first, and whose title he still refused to tell him.

"You can tell me," he pestered. "I always tell you about the books I love."

But Barker said nothing, and that bothered Purdy, too. He tried to peer in through the workshop window, but he could only see ordinary tools, pieces of wood, and paint cans. Purdy wasn't going to give up easily. He resolved to find out his friend's secret.

One day, with Barker going to the market to buy strawberries, Purdy saw his chance. Barker had needed the bicycle pump from the workshop and forgotten to lock the door. Nervously licking his lips, Purdy waited until Barker had gone out through the gate and was coasting down the hill towards the village. Then he crept into the workshop.

At first he could see nothing in the dark. At least nothing resembling a book. Cats' eyes adjust to the dark, and soon Purdy could see everything as if it were bathed in daylight. There was no book in sight, and nothing else of interest. Not until Purdy looked up. He gasped in amazement to see the pair of midnight-blue wings that hung from the ceiling. Purdy understood at once what a wonderful, one-of-a-kind friend he had. The best friend in the world, who had built wings for Purdy because he knew how badly he wanted them. Purdy was moved by the fact that Barker wanted to surprise him with such a fine present.

Delighted, he closed the workshop door. Maybe he'd be given the wings for his birthday, maybe for Christmas. It really didn't matter. Purdy could certainly wait. After all, he'd been waiting this long.

"You haven't mentioned your wings for a while," Barker remarked one morning.

"No need." Purdy gave him a knowing smile.

"So you're no longer expecting them to grow?" Barker asked.

"No," said Purdy.

"That's good," Barker sighed. He was pleased, because the mere thought of flying terrified him.

Purdy and Barker smiled at each other, like two friends who owned between them a pair of wings.

AN END AND A BEGINNING

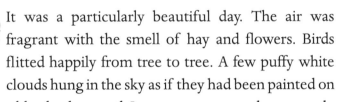 It was a particularly beautiful day. The air was fragrant with the smell of hay and flowers. Birds flitted happily from tree to tree. A few puffy white clouds hung in the sky as if they had been painted on a blue background. It was too warm to do any work, so even Barker had decided to take the day off. He was lounging under an apple tree with his straw hat over his face. Purdy made ice-cold juice with fresh water from the well. He brought the jug over and sat down beside Barker. A motor scooter hummed somewhere in the distance, but otherwise it was completely silent. And beautiful enough to make anyone's heart soar.

"There's a full moon tonight," Purdy said.

Barker didn't reply. Maybe he was asleep. Purdy couldn't be sure, because the hat covered his eyes. Only his black nose showed.

"It's been a whole year since we tried to ride our bikes to the moon," Purdy recalled with a little laugh.

Barker still said nothing. Purdy poured juice into a glass and took a long drink. It was delicious.

"Time passes," he said. There was a note of nostalgia in his voice. "Do you remember when we searched for treasure? Or when I taught you how to fish? Or when we played that ball game with Daisy Butterfield? Do you remember all that?"

Barker's breathing was deep and even. He was asleep; Purdy was sure. He gently stroked his friend's cheek.

"Time passes, but what if it comes to an end?" Purdy asked in a quiet voice. So quiet it wouldn't be heard by anyone but a very dear friend. Barker's breathing paused. Then he lifted his hat from his face and looked at Purdy with his beady brown eyes.

"What do you mean?" he asked.

"What will happen when we're no longer here?" Purdy whispered.

"Oh, this apple tree will remember us long after we're gone."

"What about after it's gone?"

"The house will remember us for even longer than the apple tree."

"What about when it falls apart and collapses?"

"This hill will still be here."

"And when the hill erodes?"

"The same sun will still be shining on this place."

"What if it stops shining? If the sun goes out, will everything end?" Purdy's eyes filled with tears. Barker sat up and put a paw

around his friend. A white wagtail waggled its tail feathers. Warm air shimmered over the lake.

"I think that's just the start of everything," Barker said.

"How do you mean?"

"The sun will go out and become dark."

"And then? What then?"

"The world will form, and life will begin on it. Birds will learn to fly, rivers will flow, and forests will grow."

"You think so? What about this hill?"

"It will rise up here, between the lake and the woods."

"And the house?"

"It'll be blue, and there will be an apple tree in the yard."

"Let me guess how it ends," Purdy said. "Underneath that apple tree there'll be a cat and a dog. They'll drink juice and they'll be best friends."

"Yes. Except, that's not the end, it's the beginning."

"Sure." Purdy laughed. "That's where it all starts."

Purdy and Barker leaned back against the apple tree and smiled at each other. Purdy poured Barker some juice and then wiped a drop of it from the tip of his nose.

"There's a full moon tonight," Purdy said. "Do you think the moonbeam path might be sturdier than last year?"

"It might be," Barker said. He glanced at his friend and smiled, then went to get two bicycles from the shed. It was Purdy's birthday, after all.